C.S. Boag is a former journalist who has also grown potatoes, driven taxis and bulldozers and worked in a hamburger bar. He has travelled many times throughout Australia and to France, speaking enough French not to die there. He was a Sydney City Councillor for six years and holds degrees from NSW and Sydney universities as well as postgraduate qualifications from Macquarie. Besides publishing short stories he has also worked as a columnist for *Woman's Day* and the *Bulletin*. He won the Walter Stone Memorial Prize for Literature in 1986. C.S. Boag lives on a small 'green' holding near Bathurst, NSW, with his wife, Judith. He has five children.

www.csboag.com

C.S. Boag

MISTER RAINBOW

in the Case of the

NIGHTMARE IN NIMBIN

XOUM PUBLISHING

Sydney

 XOUM

First published by Xoum in 2016

Xoum Publishing
PO Box Q324, QVB Post Office,
NSW 1230, Australia
www.xoum.com.au

ISBN 978-1-925143-01-0 (digital)
ISBN 978-1-925143-00-3 (print)

Cataloguing-in-publication data is available from the National Library of Australia

Word count 48,000

When Gregor Samsa awoke one morning from uneasy dreams he found himself transformed … into a giant insect.

Franz Kafka, *Metamorphosis*

Chapter 1

FIX ME OR FRAME ME

'Die, you bastard! Die!'

'Wake up, Rainbow! Wake up!'

She could be anyone – even Pandora. I lunge at her.

When she tells me what I did, she's got the marks on her neck to prove it. They aren't pretty. Murder never is.

We're on the lanai of a mansion, eating a magnificent repast beside a sea that looks like used blotting paper. I'm pretending it never happened.

'I've got two questions,' I say to Ariadne. 'What's on the news and where's the whisky?'

She has her back to the view – she's seen it before, she'll see it again and she can afford to share it. After all these years, she's still easy on the eye. She's also as hard as a bullet.

'You're not having any whisky. As for the news, in the case you chose to call the *Morgue the Merrier* there were a few innocent deaths and a lot of guilty ones; police and security rounded up what was left of the perpetrators – with the exception of someone who sounds very much like you; and Australia's safe' – she glances at me – 'at least from terrorists. Meanwhile, you're in bad shape both mentally and physically and you'll do as I say.'

I slug down my third hard black for the day. 'I'll have another one of those and get out of your hair.'

Ariadne's my childhood sweetheart who re-entered my life when I needed her. But she's worth a motza and she's also a control freak and on either count she's not for me. A ship on the horizon is so small that its passengers could be microbes. I know how they feel. I climb to my feet but my legs are spaghetti.

'I've had you sedated,' Ariadne says. 'It was in the coffee. As a result, you're experiencing a sensation known as *accidie* – a feeling of sloth, dizziness and despair usually associated with the 'flu. I've made arrangements with a clinic I happen to own and they're preparing for your admission. You'll need to stay calm while we're waiting for the ambulance.'

When she pours me another coffee, her hands are as controlled as a clergyman's conscience. 'Look, I'm doing you a favour. Your boat's at the bottom of the Harbour, the police are after you and you not only need somewhere to hide, you need help – both medical and psychiatric. Left to your own devices someone's going to end up dead and I might get dragged into it.'

Her face is swimming above me like a fish in oil.

'That's *my* pigeon,' I mutter.

'Sure. But, more importantly, it's also mine.'

The shrink leans forward, tall and cadaverous. 'Tell me about this virago, chimera, succubus, wraith – this *nemesis* you believe is following you.'

'It's not a belief – I know that she's following me for a fact.'

'It sounds to me like a case of delusionary fantasy.'

One of Ariadne's medicos has seen to my wounds while the psychiatrist – trick-cyclist, head-banger, shrink, call him what you will – is an add-on extra. I didn't have any choice. It means sleeping over at the clinic but with my boat at the bottom of the Harbour it's better than dossing in a ditch. The certificate in the frame on the wall behind him says he's a surgeon as well as a shrink.

'It sounds like you've made up your mind,' I tell him.

'So help me unmake it.'

In the silence that follows I hear what sounds like a fight to the death next door. I get off the couch and make for the exit.

Behind me the shrink says, 'It's locked.'

I unlock it with my shoulder and hurtle down the hall, to be confronted by three men in white coats. The door at the other end is too far away and the hall windows are barred like the ones in the insulting room. I take the only course open and neutralise the men in the white coats. Correction – I *try* to neutralise them. Because – courtesy of whatever they've been dosing me with – I trip over my whitesides, bang my head on the wall and end up flat on my face. Two of the nurses sit on me while the third asks, 'Want us to put a camisole on him, Doc?'

I feel like a baby's bum with the shrink's voice wafting down over me like powder. 'That won't be necessary. You can return to normal duties.' Then to me, 'If you promise to behave, Mr Nowlc, you can get up.'

I struggle to my feet. 'I'm a free citizen. You can't do this to me.'

He shepherds me back into the interrogation room. 'On the contrary, on your own admission you're no kind of citizen at all. Which means I can do pretty much what I like with you. You weren't born and have no ID: no driver's licence, credit card or private investigator's licence – not even a Medicare number. All of which means that you don't exist. While Ariadne most certainly does. I follow her orders and her orders are to fix you.'

'Fix me of what?'

'Your physical injuries are superficial while your psychological ones are far more deep-seated.'

'What psychological injuries?'

'That's for you not to know and for me to discover.'

The window overlooks the garden to the east, north's the drop-dead end of the building, south's where they park the patients, while to the west is

New South Head Road, Vauclues, the direction of freedom.

'I've managed up to now,' I tell Ariadne as we wait for the ambulance.

She shakes her head. 'You only *think* you've managed up to now. You're a pothole in everyone's road, including your own. You're resilient, I'll give you that – it's a miracle you're still alive – but the fact remains that you're faulty and you need fixing.'

'Fixing or controlling? What do you see me as – damaged goods or a hostile takeover?'

She shakes her head while her butler positions himself for trouble. 'You're a loser, Rainbow. You lost your parents and you lost me. You also lost a marriage, your aunt, too many friends, a wife and your daughter. You need help and I intend to see you get it. Otherwise you'll go down in a screaming heap and, despite all my power and my money, I'll be at risk of going down with you.'

A stepladder is standing in the corner, there's a violent altercation taking place next door and the muzak's Verdi.

'Nothing you say will go beyond these walls, Mr Nowlc,' the shrink's saying. 'Look around and all you'll see is an innocent consulting room. I'm sorry about the ladder and the half-painted walls but the clinic's a work in progress. It doesn't mean our services are anything but the best. As for privacy, I'm not taking notes. And apart from the opera – incidentally, I hope you like *La Traviata* – we're not wired for sound. So how many people have you killed?'

With his long hands clasped before him he looks like a praying mantis – make that *preying*. How many people has *he* killed?

'At last count, none. And I thought admission to joints like this was supposed to be voluntary.'

'You were signed in by family.'

'I haven't got family, apart from my daughter, and she's …'

'She's *what*?'

I shake my head. 'She wouldn't do it. Besides which she's at the police academy learning to be a cop.' My mind de-clouds. 'At least she was before Ariadne had her moved somewhere else. Imogene's got my best interests at heart so if you're saying –'

'That's precisely what I *am* saying – that you're here on your daughter's recognisance. Because, like Ms Sidonia, your daughter's concerned about your health – in particular, your mind. And in answer to your next question, yes, Imogene *has* returned to the academy.'

Chapter 2

THE WEAPON OF CHOICE

It's been a hard summer and the leaves on the trees outside look like so many little brown corpses. It might sound like I believe in signs. I don't. Once you fall for that sort of stuff you might as well believe in fairies. I'm a private eye. I deal in facts. And if you don't deal in facts, you're not dealing.

But corpses aren't all I'm thinking about as I lie on the couch staring at the manhole above me while getting an around-the-corner, side-on, how's-yer-mother third-degree from the shrink. They've drugged me but I can still hear the shrieks of the soprano – accompanied by the kind of sounds coming from next door that usually precede a murder. I imagine a wild-eyed dame waving the usual irrefutable evidence of adultery – a hotel bill in the name of Mr and Mrs Smith, a letter signed *Cuddles* or a lipstick-smudged pair of Y-fronts – and a joker doing his unlevel best to deny the undeniable. A 'domestic', the cops call it, and leave it at that. Until someone gets killed and it's not.

'Mr Nowlc?'

The weapon of choice is usually a knife while the

corpse is the one furthest from the cutlery drawer. The shrink's not a private eye, which would account for him not noticing. But I am and I have. The trouble is that the medication blunts my reactions.

'I'd appreciate your undivided attention, Mr Nowlc.'

Nowlc's not my real name but it's more than he's given me. 'How about telling me who *you* are?' I say.

'You don't trust anyone, do you? My name doesn't matter because I'm no more than a sounding board. But if you insist on a name you can call me Dr *Caligari* – as in the cabinet.'

'Could you repeat the question?'

'How long have you had this feeling?'

'What feeling?'

'The feeling that you're –' he pauses, a chair scrapes, the window slams and the sounds of the fight next door cease '– being followed.'

It's the umpteenth time he's asked this question and I give him the same answer I've given umpteen times before.

'It's not a feeling. Pandora exists.'

After the crypto-terrorists tried to destroy the Harbour Bridge in the *Morgue the Merrier* case, I found myself lying in a bed with a teardrop chandelier hanging over my head like a guillotine and Ariadne Sidonia contemplating me like Madam Defarge. All that was missing was the knitting.

'You're safe.' Ariadne might look open but she's

as accessible as a Swiss deposit box; I knew she was lying because I'll never be safe. 'Do you want to talk about it?'

I could have said: *Talk about what?*; to which she'd answer: *You know what*; to which I'd respond, *No, I don't*; and she'd say: *I think you do.* After which the dialogue would spiral off into one of those confrontations like what's happening next door. It's all about control and I don't do control. I try to remember …

It was the night of January 26 – Australia Day – and the early evening fireworks had had their moment of joy and the crowd was baying for more. Me and the bomb-whispering ex-marine Tsunami were clinging to a bomb on the Harbour Bridge when the killer came at me. I fought him off and cut the bomb free, falling into the water with it. When I surfaced it was to find Ariadne staring at me like she's staring now with an outboard motor spluttering into life – followed by darkness.

The sun streamed through the expensive window.

'What happened next?' I asked Ariadne.

She frowned at her Rolex. 'Where's that wretched ambulance? What? Oh, the bomb fell on the barge. It didn't go off and you lived because you'd managed to get it under you, detonator uppermost. You were thrown into the Harbour. I got you onto the dinghy and had you brought here. And now you're – safe.'

'What happened to the others?'

'Although the bomb didn't explode, everyone on board the barge died – including my son. My ex-lover was among the dead. I don't know what happened to …'

'Tsunami.'

Also known as Sue Mahoney, the beautiful ex-marine who helped me defuse the bomb.

'… but I imagine she died, too.'

She didn't seem all that sorry. I remember a body falling but couldn't make out whose – the bully that bashed me at school and grew up to become a madman who tried to frame the Caliphate, or the beautiful Tsunami. Which one depends on how much I wanted to fool myself. I shook my head; it was a rough night.

'What happened next?'

'As we sped away, a security boat intercepted us. But when they saw who I was, they waved me on without looking under the canvas. For several times the usual fee, a cab brought us to my house where my servants took over the heavy lifting …'

Back in the insulting room I figure I could take the shrink but that would prove nothing except that I need treatment.

'Pandora exists,' I repeat. 'What makes you think she doesn't?'

'Ms Sidonia said you were trying to kill people in your sleep. You were yelling out *Kill! Kill!* and trying to strangle her. It's known as nocto-articulation

– the revealing of hidden desires while comatose. Tallyrand once said, *Speech is a faculty given to man to conceal his thoughts.* But hiding one's thoughts is an unrealisable luxury when one's asleep, a time when Eliot – George, not T.S. – said, *Light is shed on the depth of the unspoken.*'

'You're quoting wrong and out of context.'

The shrink looks at me keenly.

'I imagine that would happen to you a lot. In the common argot, you *appear* to be as thick as wet cement but in reality you're not unintelligent. Your success as a private investigator must be due in large part to your confounding people's expectations. But I suggest you look out or you might just outsmart yourself.'

'You're making dollar judgments out of penny rumours and this is a waste of time.' For several days I've been hiding their pills and the effects are finally wearing off; I test it by getting to my feet. 'I'm not sick, I'm leaving and you can't stop me.'

The shrink shakes his head. 'If you go now, your condition will deteriorate and someone will get hurt. In which case you'd be letting down both Ms Sidonia and your daughter – not to mention the person you end up killing. What could possibly be wrong with your getting better?'

'I'm not sick.'

'Yet both Ms Sidonia and your daughter believe that you are. Let's do a deal. Pretend this is an away game and if you play ball I promise it won't go into extra time.'

'Would you mind translating that?'

'Your boat's at the bottom of the Harbour and any

friends you had have either deserted you or are dead. You've pretty much run out of options. I'm offering you a new life.'

He knows where it hurts, where the pressure points are and how to press them. I lower myself back onto the couch.

He says, 'Let's start at the beginning, shall we?'

Chapter 3

THE DEATH NEXT DOOR

It's like I've committed a crime and when I speak I'm eavesdropping on my own confession.

I was born on a hippy commune just outside the northern NSW town of Nimbin, Australia's drug capital. I had an odd upbringing – I had no schooling and there was a total absence of parental control. I'm only vaguely aware of a great deal of what happened. When I was five my mother killed herself and took my little sister with her. Dad seemed unable to cope when Mum died so with me and his current girlfriend in tow, he drove away to Melbourne, dumping me on my Aunt Ruby – his sister – on the way. Rube was a private detective who sent me to primary school but took me out when the bullying got too bad and brought me up on old gangster movies, ballet, the classics, fingerprinting, disguise and how to handle guns. I married, had a daughter, unmarried and went to live on a boat. I had a lot of enemies so Rube decided to safeguard me by expunging my existence from the records. I became a private detective. I solve crimes.

'A nice little précis,' the shrink says when I finish. 'Except it hides a great deal more than it reveals.

Let's go back to the beginning shall we, back to your very first memory.'

'I was born in a dam …' That's as far as I get.

'I'm not a Jungian, Mr Nowlc, so I don't buy the concept of awareness in foetuses or the idea of an all-purpose common memory. You don't remember your birth so don't try to fob me off with *received* information. I want your first *real* memory – what *you* recall, not what someone told you.'

'We lived in the bush, my sister was a pest and I got measles.'

The shrink sighs. '*Real* memories.'

I find myself talking; it must be the after-effects of the pills. 'I had a recurring nightmare. It involved fire, a giant figure in black and people chanting. I had trouble distinguishing dreams from reality.'

The shrink nods. 'Now we're getting somewhere.'

'*É strano! É strano! In core scolpiti ho quegli accenti!*'

The scream picks up from where the tragic heroine in Verdi's opera screeches, '*How strange! So strange! His words are carved upon my heart!*' My guess is someone's lying in a pool of blood next door and nothing's being done about it.

'How about we deal with the elephant in the room, Calvary? There was a fight next door but when I went to investigate, your goons stopped me. Now someone's dead. Deals cut two ways. Let me visit the scene of the crime and I'll tell you anything you want to know.'

The shrink sighs. 'There was no fight next door because there *is* no next door. I'll let you see for yourself but afterwards you'll have to keep your side of the bargain and talk.'

The lawn's couch – *What else would you expect from a psychiatrist,* the shrink jokes – and I blink in the sunlight like a wombat. The shrubbery's lobotomised and the joint next door – it's a Federation house, dark and ugly – is locked, barred, shuttered and clearly deserted. I stare at it, disorientated.

'You remind me of the explorer lost in deepest Africa,' the shrink says. 'Tribesmen he met said, *We're the Fukarw*ee. To which our explorer said: *Damn, I hoped you'd be able to tell me!*' The shrink pauses for effect but there isn't any so he continues. 'This is an ex-boarding school. Ms Sidonia's having it converted into a research institute.' He allows himself a smile. 'It has bars on the windows and high walls. We call it Alcatraz.'

There was a scream and the sound of a body hitting the floor – there's a corpse in the kitchen.

'Have I got to bust this door down, too?'

The shrinkwrap hauls out his hardware – he's got more keys than a grand piano. 'There's no need. But neither is there a need to investigate. The place is empty, I can assure you.'

'So now I'm hearing things as well as imagining them?'

'*You* said that, Mr Nowlc.'

'Open the door.'

He sighs, climbs the steps, crosses the verandah, opens the door, stands aside and I enter. They've taken my gat but I've still got my arms and they're out from my sides a la the late, great Jimmy Cagney.

I feint to the right, break to the left and end up in the doorway of the death room. The hall's dark but the kitchen's darker. I flick the switch but I'm still in the dark. I haul open the shutters and throw up the window.

To find the room empty and the floor even emptier.

There's no corpse, no blood, no sign of a struggle – the joint's clean. A ring-a-rosy of green benches skirts the walls but the cupboards are empty while the floor's got nothing on it but tiles. There were screams but now there aren't even echoes.

The shrink's in the doorway, smiling.

'You see? It was nothing but your vivid imagination. And now it's my turn.'

'You got me, Calvados,' I say. 'Let's go.'

I'm in a straitjacket. Calvary's goons forced me into a neck-to-waist affair that encloses my arms with a lock at the back that can only be undone by a second party. He didn't have any choice, he said, because I refused to take the pills. I lie on my back and contemplate the manhole.

'Let's start with free association, shall we? You know what free association is, I presume, Mr Nowlc?'

'Torture.'

'Clever answer. Second question: how did you feel when you witnessed the death of your mother?'

'Powerless.'

'What did you do?'
'Hide.'
'And afterwards?'
'I wanted to stop such things happening again.'
'One word.'
'Obsessed.'
'What are your feelings towards your father?'
'Blame.'
'Blame for what?'
'For the death of my mother and my little sister; for going off god knows where with a woman who wasn't my mother; for just about everything.'
'One word.'
'Abandonment.'
'What did you want to do to him?'
'I –'
'One word.'
'Death and transfiguration.'
'That's three words.'
'Rebirth.'
'Aunt Ruby.'
'Refuge.'
'Bullies.'
'Hurt.'
'Pandora.'
'Kill.'

Chapter 4

I, PANDORA

It's like trying to avoid drowning in quicksand by waving your arms about – you just sink faster. Days pass. I sleep in a dormitory to a background of the ravings of the other inmates and in the mornings return to the inquisitorial chamber for more of the same. Some nights Imogene visits – I know she visits because I hear her ask questions like: *Is he getting better?*

To which a voice replies: *It's like doing a trepan. He clams up just when we think we're making progress. It's as if he'd rather die than divulge his secret.*
What secret?
That's what we're trying to find out.

'Why can't I see my daughter when she visits?' I ask.
  'What makes you think she visits?'
  'Because I hear voices and one's hers.'
  'You're imagining the voices just as you imagined Pandora and the death next door.'

'Does she or doesn't she visit?'

'I don't live here so I don't know what happens when I'm gone. Let's just say I think it highly unlikely. So why don't you tell me about Pandora.'

'What's there to tell? Someone's following me and that's what I call her.'

'Why?'

'Why is she following me?'

'No – why do you call her Pandora?'

'When I was with Aunt Rube I studied Greek and Roman mythology: Pandora released evil into an otherwise innocent world by opening a boxful of vices. The name's appropriate because I was innocent before she arrived on the scene. Besides which I'm pretty sure that she said on one occasion, *I, Pandora.*'

'Just as you're sure there was a murder next door and you heard your daughter's voice?'

'That's different.'

'How?'

I open my eyes to find the shrink bent over his pad, scribbling furiously. 'I thought you said you weren't taking notes.'

Calvary doesn't look up. 'I'm not – I'm working something out.' He frowns for a moment and when he looks up he's triumphant. 'I've got it.'

I start drowning. 'Got what?'

'I noted early on that you're partial to wordplay – it's part of your strategy to avoid reality. You were word-playing when you made up your *cryptonym* – *Nowlc* being an anagram of *Clown*. And, consciously or unconsciously, you were word-playing when you named your nemesis.'

'But I didn't – she –'

'*I, Pandora*,' says the shrink softly. 'In an attempt to distance yourself from your problems, you came up with the kind of truth that usually only attends sleep-talking.'

'Now you're the one doing the imagining.'

'You're a most interesting case,' Calvados replies – so softly that I could be imagining that, too. 'It's a case of *Where the fuck are we* all over again, isn't it? Because, reshuffled, the letters in *I, Pandora* form a very interesting and significant word.'

'To whom?'

'To me, to you, to whomsoever you like. It's an old-fashioned word but you're an old-fashioned kind of guy.' He takes a deep breath. 'Psychiatry's come a long way since the bad old days when they locked madmen away in dungeons, chained to walls and left to grovel in their own excrement. And just as the treatment's changed so, too, has the language. Patients have become guests; we listen instead of turning a deaf ear; and we medicate them instead of beating them senseless. Where once we trundled through people's psyches in horse-drawn carts we now fly straight to the moon. What I'm referring to is a word derived from the Greek where *para* means *irregular* and *noid* is *mind*. Which adds up to a *distracted mind*.'

'I don't know what you're talking about.'

'Of course you don't. And I suppose you also don't know that *I, Pandora* is an anagram of *paranoid*.'

Chapter 5

THE MARK OF A MADMAN

It's a long time before I answer. During which I recall the unseen visits of Imogene and the non-existent murder next door and, before that, Pandora paying *her* frequent visits – which always occurred at times of greatest stress. When I return to the present Calgary's watching me closely.

'Pandora's real,' I say. 'What I call her has nothing to do with anything. Just because your name can convert into –' I think for a moment '– *A1 garlic* doesn't mean you scare vampires. The name Pandora's no more than a coincidence.'

The shrink gives me one of his looks. 'You think your phones are bugged and people are out to get you. Everyone's suspect and violence is the answer to everything. Put bluntly, you're a psychopath who might one day kill a loved one in mistake for the Devil. You describe your nemesis as "horribly scarred" one minute and "beautiful" the next. The reason for the discrepancy is Pandora doesn't exist. *Pandora*, I said, to which you replied, *Kill*. You need to be cured.'

'Only the sick need curing.'

Caligari sighs. 'And only the sane will admit they might be mad. You're sick and you need treatment.'

'Or I'm well, in which case everyone's happy.'

'That's a Band-Aid solution. And Band-Aid solutions tend to end badly, with madmen leaping off high buildings because they think they can fly or murdering a loved one because they think she's the Devil.'

He's wrong. He must be.

'There's another option,' I tell him.

'What might that be?'

'We could cut a deal.'

He sighs again. 'No more deals, Nowlc.'

'If I *am* delusional, if you're right and I need treatment before I hurt someone, I'd agree to whatever it takes – pills, electro-convulsive therapy or a lobotomy. But give me a chance to prove I'm not.'

Caligula shakes his head. 'The thing is that we don't need your agreement to treat you. You don't exist. Besides which you're basically behind bars. We can treat you however we like.'

'But what if you're wrong?'

'We can't take that risk. If Pandora *is* a figment of your imagination you need treatment. And when I advise Ariadne of my diagnosis she'll almost certainly give me the go ahead.'

'The go ahead for what?'

'Surgery.'

'But what if Pandora exists?' I persist. 'That would mean that *I'm* the one in danger. What if one day I wind up dead with a knife in my back? That wouldn't look too good on your record, would it?'

The shrink holds up his preying mantis hands. 'Only it wouldn't be on my record. You see this is a private research facility and I'm accountable only to Ms Sidonia. You *imagined* the voice of your daughter, you *believed* you heard a murder next door and you *think* you're being followed. We're not talking about a neurosis here, some minor disorder. Yours is a full-blown psychosis. You could commit murder – so sure some innocent person's Pandora that you end up killing them.'

Aeons pass. Dinosaurs tread a ferocious planet and sabre-tooth tigers roam bloodstained veldts; ice packs melt, the seas rise and there are islands. *No man is an island.* What if he's right? *Hi, Immo, I'm going to kill you.* No, no and no! Her life can't end like that. But neither can mine. Argument:

1. I'm a prisoner
2. The shrink says I need treatment
3. If he's right I'm a menace but if he's wrong I'm as good as dead
4. I don't want to die
5. I've got to find Pandora
6. But first I've got to escape.

I prepare the way. 'Okay, you're right. My aim's to protect society. Clearly I'm a danger to society and so I've got to be neutralised. I've got no choice. I agree to treatment.'

The shrink looks suddenly wary. 'Why the sudden change of heart?'

'Because I don't want to hurt anyone.'

'You're up to something.'

I shrug as much as the zoot suit allows. 'Who's paranoid now?'

It's late afternoon and streaks of cadmium orange dribble down the rungs of the ladder and onto the half-painted walls. I'm wearing a straitjacket, there are bars on the windows and the place is crawling with guards. It's a situation that would challenge Houdini. But I've got a motive, which is to prove my sanity, and I'm a great believer in motives.

The shrink's nodding.

'All right, we'll strike while the iron's hot. That's a blacksmithing term, Mr Nowlc – in order to be worked, a horseshoe needs to be malleable and at the moment you're malleable. I'll tell Ms Sidonia we're going to operate.'

'When?'

'Now.'

Description of room: six paces by six; low ceiling with manhole; barred window; one recently-patched door; couch; heavy oak desk; chair; and in the corner a stepladder. There's not much to play with but the game's on. The shrink's on the phone saying, *I have good news for you, Ms Sidonia,* when I hit him with the bad news in the form of a shoulder charge which upturns the desk. He can't say he wasn't warned. I'm a madman who could kill at any time and this is the time.

I knee the couch out of the way and using my upper body, manoeuvre the ladder into place. When I was a swan in *Swan Lake,* my arms were pinioned by feathers. It's the same now except they're no longer feathers. I lean into the ladder, climb, head-butt the manhole cover out of the way and I'm halfway into the ceiling when the door crashes open and I hear the pounding of boots. Hands clutch at my legs, my heels find a couple of heads and desperation does the rest. I twist onto my back and using positional reflex, angle west across the rafters in the direction of New South Head Road using feet, knees, shoulders, head and hands but not my arms because they're encased in the straitjacket. Alarms go off – thin, high and intermittent like drip feed in a torture chamber. From the sound of the feet hammering down the hall they've worked out where I'm headed. I change direction.

The trouble with Plan B is that the other person ends up driving. And the trouble with *this* Plan B is that the other person's mad. I crash-land into a madhouse.

They no longer call it Bedlam. A big man's wearing a tea cosy on his head; a little dame's screaming obscenities at a photograph; two men are playing poker using make-believe cards; and two girls are arguing with their backs to one another. There aren't any nurses because they've metamorphosed into guards and are looking for me. The patients are screaming. Only one – a small man with Mickey Mouse ears – isn't.

'Are you sane?' I ask him.

He nods his head. 'I'm as mad as a hatter. I committed myself even though this place is so expensive you'd have to be crazy to be here. That's how they know I'm insane.'

If I've learnt one thing from Calvary it's the fact

that the mad won't admit it; I turn my back on him. 'Unlock me.'

'Take me with you.'

'Sorry but I can't do that.'

'Then I can't unlock your jacket.'

There's no choice; feet are pounding down the hallway. 'All right, I'll take you with me. But hurry.'

The other inmates show no interest – it's as if by not acknowledging my existence, I'm not there. The coat comes off. I raise my voice. It's the voice of authority.

'I want all of you at the door on the double – *now!*'

They're mad but they're brainwashed to obey orders. There's at least twenty of them and when they're assembled at the door I raise my voice over the hubbub in the hall.

'Now we're going to play a little game.'

They nudge each other like kids in a playground – a tall man with wild hair nods, a young woman smiles and a little dame in a pinafore jigs her arms about like she's about to break into a foxtrot.

'Let's call it *The Great Escape*. When the door opens, run. People dressed as doctors and nurses will try to stop you but just remember it's part of the game. If you escape, you've earned your freedom. If you don't, you deserve to be here. Let's do it – ready, set –'

My newfound best friend tugs at my sleeve. 'It won't work. These people are all promise and no performance. It's the whispers.'

The man must be mad. 'Whispers?'

'Not whispers – *Rispers*. Risperidone. Hide in the broom cupboard and the screws will think you're not here and when they leave, I'll let you out.'

'What about you?'

'I'm madder than any of them. When the pills wear off, voices in my head tell me to kill people.' He opens the door to the broom cupboard. 'Get in.'

The only difference between him and me could be the ears. 'There's a lot of parts to what you just said and I only believe a couple of them. The trouble is I don't know which ones.' I turn to the assembled motley. '– Go!'

Chapter 6

NAMES FOR THE NEMESIS

The list takes shape and the shape's a Rorschach inkblot – the kind where you see things that aren't there. In the space headed *WHAT AM I LOOKING FOR?* I write: *Pandora*. For *WHAT DOES SHE LOOK LIKE?* I put: *Female, masked, dressed in black, carries a knife*. Then, *PROPENSITY: Murder. WHEREABOUTS: Unknown. SPECIAL INSTRUCTIONS: Avoid killing the wrong person.*

I'm on a rickety chair at a broken chart table on an unclaimed boat – one of thousands dotting Sydney Harbour – with birdlime on the superstructure, mould on the deck and angled in the water like a madwoman nodding her last. I've looked and there's no corpse, no sign anyone's been here in the immediate past or is likely to visit any time in the future. Nothing except for a notepad and pencil, an unopened bottle of port, a bit of kick in the ship's battery and a computer. I find an extension cord, rig up the computer to the 240-volt power system, take the wine and laptop topside, key in the password sticky-taped to the lid, press *ENTER* and uncork the bottle.

Under *ANYTHING ELSE?* I write: *Suspect might be armed so approach with care. LIST OF SUSPECTS: Make it as broad as you can,* Rube would insist – *cast the net wide because it could be the person least likely. Don't omit any names – you need all the fish you can fry. Pandora's been around forever but you've got to forget the little matter of age and deal with that later. First work out motive and opportunity. Imogene.*

My daughter's back at police school, Caligari said, but why should I trust him? Or is that my paranoia speaking? Paranoia's what makes me a good private eye – everyone's guilty until proven innocent. I try to shake the kid from my brainpan but I'm investigating a death and it could be mine. I've got to focus on the women in my life. First cab off the rank: Tsunami.

Word association washes up *Tsunami* but Tsunami's dead. The night on the Bridge a figure flew through the air and it might have been Tsunami but she could have survived. I Gargle the *Sydney Morning Horrible* and check the Australia Day deaths. There's no Susan Mahoney, ex-marine major, or anything like it. A figure fell from the Bridge and it might have been Tsunami but that doesn't prove rabbits. She could have slipped under the radar. I continue with the list.

Next suspect: Annie, my ex-squeeze, the heart-on-sleeve social worker. Strike one and two: she's the wrong size – too small – and too young. Only I've decided to forget *young*. Strike three: There isn't a bad bone in her. She still goes on the list. I take another swig of the hard-boiled and go back to the beginning, back to Sally, the beautiful surgeon who hired me in the case of the *Hood With No Hands*.

After that, in chronological order: Monica Best, the dame who helped me in the case of the *Horses for Corpses* – tall, blue-eyed, untrustworthy and capable of anything; Hélène Dalmatian – aka Hell and Damnation – from *Bullets at the Ballet*: amethyst-eyed and also as untrustworthy as stink; Tsunami … I complete the list but there's someone missing. *Leave out nobody, however unlikely,* Rube always said. I add the name.

Dark clouds gather, thunder ricochets across the Harbour and rain starts to fall. The wine's sour but like we sailors always say, any port in a storm. I rearrange the names in order of suspicion but it doesn't work that way so I apply reverse chronology to prevent the dice landing in any preordained order, all the time reminding myself that anything's possible. Result:
1. Sidonia, Ariadne
2. Mahoney, Sue
3. Best, Monica
4. Dalmatian, Hélène
5. Kane, Sally
6. My ex-wife Salina.

Ariadne Sidonia had me at her mercy. Question: Why would she want to neutralise me? She consorts with criminals but who in Sydney doesn't? They call killers *colourful identities* and make television series about them. Further motive – I'm a private detective who could stumble across something I wasn't meant to. A third motive is what she told me: *Left to your own devices someone might end up dead and I'd get involved.* She had the wherewithal to neutralise me so why not use it? Fourth motive: She's Pandora.

Proof positive I'm a danger is a dozen madmen – including at least one psychopath – screaming along New South Head Road, Vauclues, with doctors, nurses and guards screaming after them and cops arresting the most likely. Ariadne will organise someone to come after me – she's got the resources. She's dangerous so I put her on standby and move on to the next.

I need to see Imogene. To my surprise, she agrees.

'How are you, darling?' I ask when I call.

It's a long time before she answers and when she does it's like she's talking to a corpse. 'I told you not to contact me.'

'I was worried.'

'Maybe there's cause to worry but you brought me up to look after myself so you'll have to trust me. We can meet one more time but after that you mustn't call again.'

A lump comes to my throat. 'Of course, it was just –'

But it isn't just and when she hangs up it's as unjust as it can be. Unjust because I'm her Dad and I love her and I haven't done anything wrong. Unjust because I forgot to ask my second question which was: *Did you commit me to Ariadne's asylum and come around afterwards asking questions?* But I can't call back. Besides which she's agreed to a meeting. Besides which again, she's not Pandora and my job's to find Pandora. Like Rube always said: *Bury yourself in your work.*

Maybe I only *thought* I first met Monica Best in the case of the *Death of a Ladies' Man* – a woman on the high side of tall with beautiful eyes and even more beautiful lips. She pretended to be a coincidence but turned out to be an insurance investigator using me to do her dirty work for her. Nothing wrong with that only I don't like being used. *How come you know how to hurt people?* I asked her. *I went to finishing school,* she replied.

Some people are hard to find and others are harder. Because of her height Monica Best stands out in a crowd – I've just got to find the right crowd. She used to be in insurance but in Sydney no-one's ever what they used to be. Her size is the sticking point. Monica's well over the six-foot mark while Pandora's more or less standard. But that could be in my mind and at the moment my mind's in question. However much I want to find Monica Best it won't be a stroll in the proverbial.

Insurance companies are like sewers – they stink and the flow's all one-way. HOW – that is Home Or Wealth, the company that used to – or still does – employ Monica Best, is as tight with information as it would be with payouts. But the voice on the phone is as smooth as strawberries and ice-cream.

'Helping people is our business. Is your inquiry business or personal?'

'Business.'

'And the nature of that business?'

'It's an insurance claim – to do with personal property and therefore private.'

'I can help you with that. Do you have a file number?'

'No.'

'A name?'

I click off.

Last I knew, Imogene was in the police academy. Now she's in front of me wearing a uniform several sizes too big for her but not carrying weapons, not even a nightstick. Something's wrong.

'What is it, Chickadee?'

She was a babe in arms who became a kid, then – all too quickly – someone who made her own decisions. One of those decisions was to become a cop. It hurt at the time but you learn to roll with

the punches. We're in O'Leary's and the clientele
– drug pushers, hitmen, crooked coppers and
general lowlife – are casting covert glances at this
cop-avoiding private detective talking to a cop.
The world's been tipped on its head; nothing's
sacrosanct.

Imogene casts a look around. 'Can we go outside?'

The air in Patterson Street's foetid but it's sweet
vermouth compared to O'Leary's. We head up
Darlinghurt Road towards the Cross. Criminals
pose as taxi drivers and you can't trust anyone,
not even yourself. A spruiker bleats outside a strip
joint, a prostitute does a jig for the passing trade and
Imogene's got a problem. Correction: a problem's
got Imogene.

'I can't say what it is,' she says, 'or you're likely to
go off like that gun you once showed me – half-
cocked. I'm no longer at the academy.'

Chapter 7

A MESSAGE FOR MONICA

'Do you need my help?' I say.

'From what I hear, you're the one needing help.'

'What have you heard?'

'At the academy we're kept apprised of any news involving the *Force Field* – that is, what's happening regarding the police outside the academy. One item caught my attention because Ariadne Sidonia's name was attached to it – a breakout from some psych facility followed by a hunt for the instigator. I don't have to be Sherlock Holmes to know the instigator was you.'

I can't pretend we walk on in silence because the Cross is never silent – sirens wail, tyres screech, people scream and you can hear the guns go off if you're listening. I cut back to the action.

'You tell me the academy's not going well.' I can't say I'm not pleased; I've never liked cops and I like the idea of my daughter becoming one even less. 'What's the problem?'

Imogene shrugs her shoulders. 'There was an incident, they're holding an inquiry and while they're holding their inquiry, I'm *persona non grata*.'

'Come on Immo, give me a clue.'

'Giving you a clue is giving you the answer.'

I change the subject. 'How's Mum?'

'I'm not staying at home if that's what you're asking. They put me somewhere but I can't tell you where it is. I tricked my way out to see you because I knew you'd make inquiries if I didn't.' She glances at her watch. 'I've been out too long, I need to get back.'

I've got to ask and I've got to ask fast.

'What do you know about Pandora?'

She looks at me strangely. 'Your so-called "nemesis"? Only that I've never seen her.'

She puts quotes around the word so I don't pursue it. 'At least you're still alive, Immo.'

'What's that supposed to mean?'

'Fathers worry.'

'There's nothing to worry about.'

Which tells me one thing.

And that is that there is.

My ex, Salina, opens the door and stares daggers at me. I imagine her *throwing* daggers at me and get in my two-bob's worth before she can reach for the weaponry.

'I've got a couple of questions, Sal.'

'What, like: *Do you regret meeting me?* To which the answer's a resounding *yes.* Or: *Do I want you dead?* In which case the answer's *yes* again. You're never going to get out of my life are you, Rainbow?

It's like you're *tailing* me. Although I believe a better word would be *stalking*.'

'I thought that *you* might be stalking *me*.'

Salina stares at me for a good minute. A minute's a long time when Salina's staring at you. It's like being face to face with a psychopath – you begin the countdown to death. Salina's got sharp nails and maybe also somewhere there's a knife.

But instead of trying to kill me she starts laughing. At first it's a slow laugh but then it gathers momentum and becomes a shrill laugh, a kookaburra's laugh, the kind you might hear in a ghost train, the kind that chases you to the grave, and she's still laughing long after I've gone. I know because I can hear her a block away, even though I've got my hands over my ears.

Bury yourself in your work and be thankful for large mercies – Imogene's alive and there's nothing you can do to help her unless she asks. The chest tags that HOW – the insurance company – issues to staff aren't rolled gold. They haven't even got feature measurements or fingerprinting – just a face and number. I bump into an employee, pat his chest as I step away from him, insta-camera his ID, return it without him being aware I borrowed it and take the result to Ace Mollema.

Ace was one of the kids on the funny farm – the name we kids gave to the collective at Nimbin – except that he left some time before me. One day he was there, the next he wasn't. He became a spook – a spy with Australia's intelligence agency, ASIO – and I last saw him when I needed a fake passport; last spoke to him when I discovered he'd dudded me. I ask him to make a copy of the ID with my face on it. He still feels guilty so he does me the favour. He's also got something on his mind.

'Do you ever think about the funny farm?' he asks.

'Just the one copy,' I say.

'When my grandparents took me away they called it a *kin*-nap.'

'How long will it take?'

'I'll have it ready for you within the hour.'

However much security people have got, it's always going to have holes in it and when I enter the HOW Tower wearing the uniform from the Prop Shop and waving my fake pass the guard doesn't take his eyes off his comic. And at the second hurdle – the one where you actually need to look like who you're pretending to be – when I display the brown paper parcel, the dame looks up from her crossword.

'What's *Basic instinct, the crime of being someone else,* in two words – eight letters and five?'

'It's *id* and *robbery* – the answer you're looking for is *identity theft*.'

She smiles as she clicks open the door. 'That gets you into the holograph.'

HOW rents floors number thirty-eight to fifty and I start on thirty-eight, entering the lift in the company of a bunch of workers saying, 'Parcel for Monica Best'. Which gets me frowns and shrugs all the way to the top, where I'm still saying, 'Parcel for Monica Best'.

An ugly little joker looks up from a sausage machine behind the cafeteria counter.

'You mean Monica *West* – as in: *The men she rejects make Monica West the best?* You're too late, mate, she's gone.'

I turn to go. Always turn to go. 'Sorry to have bothered you.'

'Hold on a moment there, Hotfoot.' He comes around the counter mopping his hands. 'Nice lady, Monica, despite her height – always a kind word for the little man. What do you want?'

'I've got a message for her – in fact, a parcel – and this is her last known address.'

'Last known to you maybe but not to me.'

The clock's running but I can't appear to be running with it because that's when they smell a rat. People are scared of rats. I start for the lift.

'I don't have to do the delivery.'

'Jeez – just a minute, will you?' I wait; he's keen to talk; always wait when they're keen to talk. 'Monica was beautiful and a top operator. Nice person, too. But she had her enemies. When things went bad I overheard people in the lunch queue saying she deserved it.' He pauses. 'There might have been something else, too; the feeling she was – well, different.'

'I'd better go.'

'Her Waterloo was a disputed claim for insurance. The matter went to court but it was her word against the claimant's – a Greek woman whose husband was a conman.'

The sequel to *Death of a Ladies' Man*.

'It would have helped if a certain private detective had given evidence but he disappeared like he never existed, leaving Monica to pick up the pieces. The judge didn't give an inch. When he ordered the company to pay, Monica's fellow workers actually cheered. When she was sacked, she sued for wrongful dismissal but she got no support.'

'I'll mark the parcel *Address unknown*.'

'But other people's enemies are my friends so I gave my condolences and we kept in touch. She got a job but not in insurance because the company blacklisted her. What's in the parcel?'

'Money, I think.'

'I know where you can find her.'

'I'm a delivery boy not a private detective. It's not my job to find her.'

'You don't have to. I can tell you where she went.'

Chapter 8

THE KARATE KILLER

He's built like a Mack truck and comes at me fists first, a giant with a face that didn't evolve along with the rest of him. I dance to the right but that's when I discover he's a *dan* – a black belt in karate – his beautifully executed *mawashigeri* – roundhouse kick – catching me as I do the splits. He follows with a full-frontal kick – a *maegeri* – but I'm ready for that, too, and a *glissé* with arms transposed gets me out of the way. It's nice to see the kind of damage ballet can do to a *dan*.

'*Kiai!*' he yells, which roughly translates as: *You bastard!*

'The same to you,' I reply and headbutt him in the gut.

We're in Aces, the nightclub that lawmakers are always going to crack down on but never get around to because it's part of their investment portfolio. Its façade features nice people smiling sweetly at each other while inside it's wall-to-wall drugs.

All I did was mention the name Monica Best.

It's daylight so the joint's empty if you don't count the thug. He comes at me again, this time with murder in his eyes where before it had only been mayhem. But I'm ready for the *ashibarai* – the leg-sweep – making myself as small a target as possible for a six-foot-something detective. *Bring it to a conclusion,* I tell myself. *You're looking for information, not for trouble.* He's got his eyes on my *chudan* – my mid-section – which means he's got another target – my knees or my head – because he wants to finish it, too.

Always beware the *gyakuzuki* – the reverse punch. It's a short-travel hit and delivery can occur from a standing position or with the deliverer retreating or advancing. Again he's looking elsewhere which means he's going to go for my midriff. The standard counter's the kick that weakens the punchline. He's ready for it but that's all he's ready for. I do a *grand jeté,* legs apart and arms spread like I'm flying – I can almost hear Hérold's music for *La Fille Mal Gardée,* almost see the dancer Alain as I snap my foot in the pug's face and he goes down. It's like kicking a habit – it might be hard but it's well worth the effort. I pour water over him out of a bucket from the bar.

'Where is she?'

'I don't remember.'

The pressure point's just below the ear, the one that results in paralysis or – if I'm not careful – death. Just as fat men possess the same skeleton as thin ones, the placement of nerves never varies. I remember the shrink's warning: *One day you'll kill someone you don't intend to.* I don't ease off.

'What did she do here?'

'She bounced.'

'Why did she leave?'

'The boss's girl thought she was after the boss so she spread rumours.'

'Where did she go?'

'How would I know?'

'Because you want to live.' I fight back the urge to really hurt him. 'Where did she go, Spitgut?'

She got a job in a rival club, he says, but that didn't last long, either. *Where did she go after that?* The thug produces a thug's leer. *When you're as tall a poppy as that dame, the only way to go is down.* I thump him in the guts and dump him.

You hear of ugly drunks ending up in the gutter but not beautiful women. That's because by the time they're on the greasy slide to nowhere they're no longer beautiful. I decide to press two lemons with the one squeezer and go in search of Annie.

Annie's a former squeeze but right now she's just another ex, yet another dame who's better off without me. She tends to the homeless and I find her in a park in Darlinghurt.

'Hi, Annie.'

She's crouched over a bundle of rags. She risks her life for others but anyone could be Pandora and she's not about to jump at a voice she'd prefer to forget.

'I'm looking for someone.'

She doesn't look up. 'You're always looking for someone, Rainbow. If it's not a suspect, it's the love of your life.'

I stretch the truth. 'This one's at risk of dying.'

'Everyone's at risk of dying – that's one thing I know better than anyone. But before you go, help me get Xavier into the van.'

Xavier's a bundle of dirty linen that stinks of hard liquor and grunts.

'Her name's Monica Best,' I say as I help with the lift. 'She's tall and very beautiful.' Already Annie hates her and Annie hates nobody with the possible exception of me; she slams the door hard in case my hand's in the way. 'The reason I'm after her is she might be Pandora.'

Annie shoots me a funny look. 'Your so-called nemesis? Don't tell me you're still living in the threat of shadows and the hope of eternal love. When are you going to accept that Pandora doesn't exist and nor does the love of your life? No-one will ever commit to you, Rainbow, because you can't commit to yourself. Now if you'll excuse me I have work to do.'

She's wandered off the main track; I steer her back on. 'Where would I find her?'

'Who – Pandora or this Monica woman?'

'Either or both.'

'If I tell you, will you leave me in peace?'

'I promise.'

Annie climbs behind the wheel. 'She's at The Three Sisters.'

'Why would she be at a women's refuge? Monica's not afraid of anyone.' Annie starts the engine; there's time for one last question. 'Tell me it isn't you, Annie.'

There's time for the question but not for the answer.

She's already driven away.

If you're looking for a straight-line job avoid detecting. Because in detecting the best way from A to B is mostly by way of Z. This is due to:

1. Red herrings – which distract the investigator because, like their name suggests, they're brightly coloured and stink; and

2. Baseless assumptions.

Watching Annie go leaves a hole in my heart as big as The Gap, the cliff at Watsons Bay that people jump off when they're in a bad way. We used to be lovers but we'll never be lovers again. Annie said I'm married to my work and maybe she's right. But going by what she said about Pandora, she left me because I'm a basket case. But that's a baseless assumption and finding Pandora will prove it. I hotfoot it down South Darling, up Cleveland to Broadway, past the City Morgue to The Three Sisters.

Chapter 9

THE THREE SISTERS

I work my way to a spruce tree on a rise overlooking the refuge and while waiting for inspiration try to talk myself out of Monica Best. This is the *delusional phase* in detecting and goes something like:

1. She's too young – Pandora's been following me since before Monica was born
2. She's too tall and
3. She's got no motive.

Think positive. Forget her height and age. She was an insurance agent, hired to track down frauds. I came across her in the *Death of a Ladies' Man*, waiting for me behind locked doors. A strong dame who knew her way around self-defence, which puts her in the ballpark. Setting aside height and age, what could be a possible motive? She could hate men and this man in particular. But that's a stretch of the imagination and I don't do stretches of the imagination. Or she's mad and the mad don't need motives. Which is pretty much what the shrink said about me.

What bounces her out of the reckoning is her age. Monica postdates Pandora, which means that at thirty-something – even if she's pushing forty

– Monica's still too young. But that's a red herring if not also a baseless assumption. So forget *young* and return to *motive*. Why would Monica follow me, haunt me, track me down and put me in fear for my life?

Why does anyone follow anyone? Why do stalkers stalk? Out of hatred, anger, jealousy? Whatever it is, they don't want the object of their affections to be with anyone else. *I'd rather you were dead* is the usual sentiment. Because their so-called *love* is a sense of ownership where the mate's regarded as a possession. But that's not why Monica would be on the follow. We've got no history unless it's a history I'm not aware of. Apart from which, she's not the one doing the following – I am. Return to motive:

1. Love – discount love
2. I've hurt someone close to her or she thinks I have – an outside chance
3. Mistaken identity; I'm a six-foot-something private detective that dresses bad – discount
4. Anger – but at what?
5. Other.

I could be talking about myself. How can I not be a stalker when I'm hanging around a women's refuge in the middle of the night, looking for a woman?

Any one of those cars pootling along Grebe Point Road could contain Pandora. There are too many suspects and too little time. But cutting corners leaves holes in the net that could let in a shark. I've got to follow up *all suspects* – including the most unlikely – and I've got to do it thorough. If there's no Pandora, it means I'm mad. Monica's a suspect and there's someone behind the bush.

The bush is an oleander – pink-flowered and poisonous – while the figure's grey-tracksuited and even more dangerous than the bush. I don't have to be a mind reader to know what he's after. Which means it's business as usual at the refuge.

There's the familiar *click-clack-click* of bolt cutters as he severs the wires but no alarms go off because they're neutralised. He's wearing a head-mounted torch with its beam directed at the fence so I can't make out his features. All I know is that he's big. But at night, everyone's big, like the bats of my childhood. *If they get in your hair, you have to cut off their legs,* my mother warned. *If you need the scissors, they're beside the bed.* In my five-year-old mind those bats were vampires.

My reaction's slow because I didn't expect him. I forgot the number one danger in detecting, the red herring. I thought the figure with the bolt cutters was a break-in because I was supposed to think that. I thought the target was someone in the refuge when all the time it was me. I was *meant* to be watching the man with the bolt cutters – that's why he was there. I'm a sitting patootie.

There's no time to respond. Thug number two's got me pinioned, his hands clenched at my chest, and I feel my stored air diminish as the figure at the fence starts our way. When you're caught by surprise you feign helplessness to make your attacker relax. But that's what the Squeezer's expecting because he's a trained attacker. Which means he's ready for the relax ploy, I'll run out of breath and I'll be dead. But that's before anger takes over. Anger at my not realising what they were up to; anger at being tricked. And my anger neutralises common sense like the figure at the fence has neutralised the alarm. Instinct takes over. And that's what saves me.

I lock my elbows and the Squeezer's arms find themselves wrapped around steel. I twist out of his clutches but he's ready, his fist raised to deliver the death blow just as Fence Man arrives. All thought deserts me and I'm left with nothing but the blind, savage will to survive. Something tells me to duck as the bolt cutters scythe over my head, as big as a battleaxe and just as lethal. The Squeezer screams as the cutters crunch into his face. Then Fence Man's onto me.

At times like these your mind functions on two levels. On one level I'm coordinating my responses to my attackers while on another, more conscious, level I'm trying to work out who they are. Because knowing who they are is how I'll survive. That's how I'll know if they want to kill me or just keep me for questioning. The answer decides the mode and ferocity of their attack and therefore my counter to it. I feint to the left, fall and slide down the slope as Fence Man comes after me.

This is not some random event – a raving lunatic and his mate after the maniac's missus. Nor is it a couple of passers-by who happen to be in the vicinity. The wire-cutting exercise was a warm-up while the assault's the main event. They were tailing me when I was with Annie – possibly before. They heard her direct me to The Three Sisters, worked out their plan of action, picked up a pair of bolt cutters if they didn't already have them and were waiting when I arrived because they had wheels while I didn't.

But that doesn't tell me *who* they are or *why* they're after me. *You're imagining things,* the shrink said. Only I'm not imagining this. I'm on the ground, the Squeezer's somewhere in the spruce needles and Fence Man's coming for me again.

I get to my feet but the needle-covered ground's slippery and my footing's uncertain. My attacker's head torch has slipped about his neck, up-lighting his face. I don't know him which means he's an out-of-towner. A bent cop? A crony of some crook I crossed? A hitman? He could be any of a number of criminals or an accomplice. He's male so he's not Pandora. So who is he and why is he after me?

When you're under attack, never over-think. Thinking's dangerous. Think and you lose focus, think and you waver. The thug senses my indecision and, grabbing me by the hair, drags me to the ground. With the advantage of certainty he's astride me like the fifth horseman of the Apocalypse, his raised arm outlined against the moon, half-lit face triumphant. He's Death and he's got me. The arm begins its descent.

He's not keeping me for questioning.

Darkness is death, death darkness. There's a flash

– the kind of light that was there when the world began – then darkness. I manage to twist so the slicing-down hand catches the point of my shoulder instead of my throat. It's the best I can do. The shoulder goes numb and I roll further down the hill. From somewhere come the strains of *Death and the Maiden* – the string quartet in D minor. Did Schubert call it that because of its dying fall – the death drop? I glimpse something between my attacker and the moon. It could be my imagination or it might be a bat – there are fig trees around here and bats like figs. I steel myself for the death blow.

Chapter 10

BODIES ARE MY BUSINESS

A cat's got nine lives but a private detective's got none. A gumshoe's a dead man walking, surprised to wake up in the morning and find he's still alive. He treads the shadows – a wraith, a spectre, a phantom. And I'm one step along even from that. I don't exist. And now I'm about to exist even less.

I'm held down by one thug while the third – the one outlined against the moon – arrives like pestilential rain. *If they get in your hair, chop off their legs – the scissors are next to the bed.* I grapple among stones, twigs, leaves – a child scrabbling for scissors – and my hand closes on the bolt cutters. I raise my arm to get the cutters between me and the figure coming at me out of the sky while trying to dislodge the figure astride me. *He was clutching a pair of bolt cutters – he must have been breaking into the refuge when he was surprised.* I feel the thud of a body, the bolt cutters crash onto my chest, then there's silence. Silence and utter darkness.

'Rainbow!'

Rainbow was the name my mother gave me when I was born and a rainbow appeared in the sky. *It's a sign!* she said, although she didn't have a clue what of. *My little Mister Rainbow,* she crooned. She must have been as mad as a tailless wallaroo even then. I hear the voice from the past croon, *'Rainbow!'*

I'm dead and I'm hearing voices. Dying smells of blood, decaying leaves, rotten spruce needles and dirt. Let me lie here and decay, part of the Great Plan – death and configuration. Or should that be *trans*-figuration? And if transfiguration, what does *that* mean? If *rebirth*, why not say so?

'Mum,' I hear myself reply.

'Rainbow!'

She's giving me the kiss of Death, her cold mouth pressed hard against mine like she needs to devour me. It's Pandora come to claim me. I struggle but Death's astride me, her weight too great for me to move. My shoulder hurts, my head, my chest, my face. My lungs are bursting because my mouth is blocked by this succubus crushing me. The pressure intensifies, unaccountably eases, then intensifies again. I sense a pattern here and I can do patterns. I count five-second intervals and realise what it means. It's the Silvester method of cardio-pulmonary resuscitation – CPR. Which means that it's not the kiss of death at all but the kiss of life. I open my eyes. It's her.

I didn't check face, clothes, pockets of the corpse. When there's a body that doesn't belong to you, you get away fast. Because when people find bodies they start looking for who made them that way. I ought to know. Bodies are my business.

I don't know how far she lugs, drags, half-carries me. One rib's fractured where the Squeezer did his work, my shoulder aches, a leg defies straightening and my face is bruised. There's nowhere that doesn't hurt. Pandora's dragging me along a footpath when her foot catches on a root, a streetlamp or a bench and she stumbles and falls. That's when she sees one of my shoes and my fedora are missing. And that's when I see that my rescuer isn't Pandora at all but Monica Best.

'We can't leave any evidence,' she says. 'I need to go back.'

She's away for an eternity, during which I drop in and out of consciousness. Bats circle and I don't know if they're imagined or real. Footsteps hurry past and there are cars. I'm dead. Then I'm alive again as hands force the shoe back on my foot, cram the hat on my head and get me to my feet.

'Christ, you're heavy,' she says as she carries on dragging.

After a while she stops again. Next to us I make out a fence and decide that the world must be made of fences – fences to keep people in, to keep them out. Tall, short, wire, wood, corrugated-iron, stone or brick – *fences, defences and offences*. Monica's breathing hard, a winded animal, blown.

'Why were you at the refuge?' she manages to ask.

'I was following someone.'

'You were lucky I was there.'

'You were the someone I was following.'

Cases should be discrete – separate – but at least two have become joined: the hunt for Pandora and the one where someone's hunting me.

Early-morning workers hurry past wearing Hi-Viz jackets and carrying lunch boxes. Headlamps impale us and a cyclist wobbles off the footpath onto the road. You can't stagger about inner-city streets in the early hours of the morning looking like us without someone calling the cops. We get going again.

We're on a patch of grass overlooking Grebe Point Bay, the weak sunlight glistening on the oars of a rowing shell slicing through the water, a black dog galloping along the bank beside it, barking. *One-two*, the coxswain calls. *Yap-yap*, goes the dog. Monica gets her wind back.

'Why were you following me?'

Don't answer questions – ask them. 'Did you know me before I met you?'

'How could I know you before I met you?'

In *Death of a Ladies' Man*, a dame called Annabel Franklin was in danger and I rang the bell to another flat to gain access to her unit block. It turned out to be Monica's. As an insurance investigator, she was following Annabel so it was natural she'd be in the flat above. It was also possible she was lying in wait for me. But why would she save me if she was Pandora? I put the question.

'Once you were a voice on the intercom, then – when you opened the door – a girl with a gun. Did you already know me? Did you have a grudge against me, as well as the gun?'

'You tracked me down just to ask me *that*?'

The dog splashes into the water but the scullers keep to their dead-straight line. Like the rowers I mustn't allow myself to be deflected. 'Second question: why were you at the refuge if you weren't trying to escape from someone?'

'I was a guard at the refuge, not an inmate. I was on watch, heard a noise and went to investigate. When the man at the fence tried to get away I went after him and came across you getting killed.' She gives voice to my thoughts. 'Why would I rescue you if I was trying to hurt you?' Then, 'Who were they?' And, when I don't answer that question either, 'You need to see a doctor.'

'No way. A doctor would report me to the cops; the cops would link my injuries to the death at the refuge; and I'd be arrested, given an identity, charged, found guilty and do time.'

She interrupts, 'Make that *deaths* because there were two of them. Which reminds me – I need to get back before someone finds the bodies.'

I get to my feet. 'You've been following me, haven't you?'

She brushes the grass clippings off her jeans; she also brushes away my question. 'I thought you said that *you* were the one doing the following.' Her eyes return to the scullers – the dog's splashing back to shore, its barking reduced to yelps – then back to me. 'Seeing you refuse to see a doctor, I'll leave you with Mildred.'

Chapter 11

TOO CLOSE FOR COMFORT

Mildred's on the far side of sixty, limps and lives in a dungeon under Grebe Point Road. I don't ask where she got the limp.

'We have been in the wars, haven't we?' she says.

I know her profession by the number of the pronoun and the concern. 'You're a nurse, aren't you?'

'Lie on the couch.' She fills a bowl with water to which she adds gentian violet after which she kneels beside me. 'And in answer to your question, no, I'm not a nurse – I'm a double-certificated sister retrenched to make way for a kid who does nothing but sit in the corridor avoiding all patient contact and playing with computers. You don't know anything about hospitals.'

She applies the disinfectant. It hurts. She's right. I don't.

I haven't got long, no more than a pig's whisper. I've got to think fast at a time when I'm having trouble thinking at all. The shapes of pedestrians wobble over glass bricks in the ceiling and photos sit on the Radiola: old pictures, young pictures, sepia pictures – coloured and monochrome – and when Mildred leaves the room I study them. There's one of a young nurse, a middle-aged nurse, an old nurse – sorry, *sister*. But a different kind of sister to the one my mother killed. An older woman with a soul's curse on her, an *angry* woman. It's life in fast-forward – Mildred as a young woman in the company of an older woman who looks pretty much like Mildred does now; Mildred holding a baby; Mildred with a child; Mildred and Monica. *Ashes to ashes, death and regeneration.* There's something about the background in the Mildred-and-child photograph.

But it's not Mildred's background I need to concern myself with – it's mine. I'm on the right track but I need to cover all bases. All the clichés. I rewrite my list. There are more suspects – a lot more if I don't scratch dark horses like Rory's ex-wife, Janet Q. Peters; Lisette Priée, the ballet dancer; the pianist with the multi-coloured eyes, Gertrude Match; and my old mate Harry's alleged or otherwise squeeze, Denise, also known as *de niece* – Babychino. And why shouldn't Pandora be someone I don't know, the unknown follower?

After Mildred leaves, I carry the photograph to the light. Behind the two figures are rolling hills. After that – day after day – I force myself to do press-ups – *one-two, one-two* – my legs and body straight and the threadbare carpet hard under my fingertips, screaming silently with the pain in my arms. *One-two, one-two.* As soon as I can, I start circling the dungeon like a prisoner, keeping track of the laps – doubling, tripling and quadrupling them. All the time marking off the days – *one, two.* And at the end of the seventh day calling a halt.

'I've got to go.'

'But you're not well enough.'

'No-one's ever well enough, Mildred, but it doesn't stop them going.'

The phone number's not perched on its hind legs begging to be dialled but I'm not a pet owner, I'm a detective who's run out of dead-men's mobiles so I use a call phone. A termagant answers.

'What do you want?'

'It's not *what* I want – it's *who*. I'm after Monica Best.'

The valkyrie's got a stock line and she uses it. 'There's no-one here of that name.'

'She's not an inmate.'

Another stock line, 'We don't call them inmates, they're guests.'

'She's not a guest – she's a guard. And I'm not a danger man – I'm a friend.'

'I'll see if she's here.'

'You're too close.'

I move away.

'I don't mean too close to *me*, I mean to this Pandora business.'

We're in a Likeheart coffee shop and the place is crowded. It feels like normalcy. I like normalcy. You can't get hurt in normalcy.

'And before you ask,' Monica continues, 'a jogger found the bodies and the police visited the scene. They questioned me but I denied everything. Despite my denials I'd be a person of interest except they weren't all that interested – either in me or in the bodies. The killers were members of the Irish Republican Army.'

I nod. 'In other words, they had no ID but Interpol had their fingerprints which they kindly provided to the local *gendarmerie*. But what are the IRA doing in Sydney hanging around a women's refuge?'

'That's what I was about to ask you.'

I change the subject. 'What happened to the cops?'

'Jenny – that's the name of the woman in charge at the refuge – wouldn't let them in without a warrant so I had to go out to them. They walked me over the crime scene – from the hole in the fence to the place where the jogger found the bodies. They said they had evidence that I was implicated but they weren't interested because the men were IRA and dead. They still wanted to know why I didn't report it but I said there was nothing to report. They asked about you.'

'Why would they do that?'

I'm what's known in the trade as *layering*

– superimposing what *might* have happened onto what the witness is saying. Monica was interviewed by the cops. Check – it's a fact not in dispute. But why were they there? First possibility: Monica contacted them. With that in mind I superimpose a second layer: that the cops didn't ask about me – Monica volunteered the information. Third layer, following on from layers one and two: she's here to implicate me. Fourth layer: she's wired.

She shakes her head. 'I can read your thoughts as clearly as if your head were made of glass. For God's sake, I *rescued* you – you have to trust me. The police only asked about you because of your footprints.'

'Which means they must also have found yours. Which means you lied either to me or to them when you said that you didn't investigate.'

'I was trying to cut corners.'

'Whose – theirs or mine?'

'I'm not trying to entrap you, Rainbow. The cops aren't after you for the simple reason I didn't tell them about you. Look around – do you see anyone suspicious? I lied to you once and I want to make up for it.' She takes a deep breath. 'There's something I haven't told you.' There's always something they haven't told you. 'It's this.'

From her pocket Monica pulls a rough-cast affair the size of a glasses case. It's a coarse-weave thing of violet-coloured cloth, roughly sewn around a thatch of straw. When I turn it over, a face stares back at me, a leering face with a patch of hair askew on its forehead, a crooked mouth and criss-crosses of black cotton for eyes. The eyes make the doll look unconscious or dead. Someone's slashed its calico chest. The doll brings back memories but I don't know what of. All I know is that it's beckoning me to my past. Monica's fidgeting.

I waggle the doll. 'Where did you find this?'

'At the scene of the crime – on the hillside outside the refuge. I didn't tell you about it before because – well, because of what I said: you're too close and this might make you closer. You could overplay its significance.' She shakes her head. 'Look, it's just an innocent doll, probably dropped there by a kid.'

I think back to the night outside the refuge – one body on the ground and Monica in the process of making it two. It was too dark to see dolls.

'*When* did you find it?'

'I went out at first light to cover your tracks and see if either of us had left any clues. I used to be an insurance investigator, remember, so I know all about clues. I was smoothing down the soil and scattering leaves about when I found it.'

'It's clean. Did you brush it? It would be a natural thing to do – people like things to be clean.'

'No, that's how I found it.'

Chapter 12

BURN CITY

Simeon Samson's behind his desk with a gun at his head and it's my gun. With the sinking of the old tub, the *Wooden No*, along with all my weaponry, I've had to make do with the odd spanker from nefarious sources. The one I'm wielding is a Golightly – otherwise known as an Astra Cub 2000. There's no safety on the grip and it's pretty well obsolete but beggars can't write their own orders and it doesn't make much of a bulge in my jacket. There are a thousand ways to get past security and I only had to use one of them.

In trying to prove I'm not a psychopath, I've got to move a lot faster than usual. My old mate Rory's ex-wife, Janet Q. Peters, is worth a visit; the dancer I was brought up with, Lisette Priée, ditto. The pianist with the multi-coloured eyes, Gertrude Match, is a long shot but long shots can still hit the target; likewise Denise, also known as de niece

– Babychino. Not to mention Hell and Damnation, the dame from the *Bullets at the Ballet* caper, real name – if anyone's ever got a real name – Hélène Dalmatian.

So like I say, in detecting terms I'm well over the speed limit – in this game you've got to go steady or risk kicking the ball into touch. But I've got no choice. Pandora exists – I've got to keep reminding myself of that or accept that I'm mad. I sense her around the next corner and behind the last, a dark shape on the edge of the crowd, a figure in an otherwise empty corner of my consciousness, an ever-present menace. I repeat: I've got to prove she's real or accept that I'm mad. The doll in my pocket's clean but that doesn't mean Monica Best is. She's still on my shopping list.

Sydney's Burn City, Nero's Rome, a place where punters have got to be pond hoppers just to survive. Hélène Dalmatian could have gone back to her native stomping ground – France – or simply changed her name and address and stayed. Which is why I'm visiting *Natality, Mortality and Misery Inc* – also known as the Department of Burps, Debts and Massages – and holding a gun to Simeon Samson's head.

'Why the gat?' he asks.

'Because I want some information and you're reluctant to provide it.'

'Our superiors – not to mention Australia's

security agencies – watch us like echidnas hang around ants and if we deviate from the norm *in the slightest* we're hauled off for questioning. They're not sympathetic to the leaking of information.'

'That's why I've got the gun – it makes me even less sympathetic than they are. Do it.'

Reluctantly Samson fingertips his way into forbidden territory – like bugs are coming out of the computer and crawling all over the keyboard. *Password,* the screen asks – he provides it. Then: *Reason for inquiry* – he provides that, too. After which: *On whose authority are you asking?* He types in a name. Followed by one last chance to stay clean: *Are you sure?*

He shakes his head. 'I'm dead.'

'We're all dead, get used to it.' I jam the barrel hard into his head. 'Find the name,' I say, a touch more savagely than I need to.

Everyone in Australia's on a grid called an IGU – an Intelligence Gathering Unit. The security people can deny it till they're pink, blue or violent in the face but everything, and I mean everything – names, nicknames, friends, enemies, relatives, ages, interests, addresses, sexual proclivities, what you had for breakfast and the state of your kidneys – goes back to base. There's a bit of privacy but people with Samson's seniority can override it.

'Faster,' I tell him.

'Here he is: *Flax – Albert,*' he says. 'That's the name of the sugar daddy, right? *Ex-Olympian, financier, deceased.*' He leans back, wiping his palms on his trousers, job done. 'There's a heap of detail – awards for service to society, contacts with crooks, unproven allegations of this, that and the other, no relatives, blah-blah-blah, list of girlfriends, the last one being *Dalmatian, Hélène* – subsequently rebadged as *Helena Dannazione*. Satisfied?'

He's forgotten his fear in the thrill of the chase. He's also forgotten his brains.

'Not by a long shot, Delilah,' I growl. 'Tap dance your way to *Helena Dannazione*.'

In my book there's no such thing as coincidence. My legs are rubber as I leave the building, climbing the staircase from Samson's hidey hole, going down multiple corridors with little glass cubicles leading off them. I finally pass a security that's no longer interested because I'm leaving. Before saying bye-bye to Samson I placed a bullet on his mouse pad – a .23 slug the size of a gnat.

'A little memento of my visit. So that when they're giving you the third, fourth or fifth degree for breeching security, you'll tell nobody nothing except that it was all your idea.'

The lawn's freshly mown, there's a sign on the newly-painted fence saying *BUY ME* and the joint looks as innocent as a new-born ferret. But there's someone inside – I know it for a fact because of the curtains. I'm dressed for anonymity – grey tracksuit, even greyer shoes, forage cap turned backwards. The curtains are open. I continue up the street without turning my head.

Sydney's all about real estate – call it real *astute* – which makes realtors the new elite. From being the dregs of society they've risen to the top of the oil can because selling houses has become one of the black arts of success. And part of that art is keeping the curtains closed. That way no-one gets to see in without an appointment; buyers beg for admission; and the agents get their *Lo and behold!* moment when they throw open the curtains exclaiming, *Let there be light!*

At the end of the block I chuck a left and head down Prime. Due to the booming property market Browntown's shifted gear from chugalug to second – there's no longer a lot of wrecked cars in the gutter, the dog poo's been cleared away and people pull T-shirts over their singlets before going for a walk. I climb the back fence.

It was meant to be no more than a house call. Rube's files – the ones containing all her cases, her diary, codes and advice – is in a filing box behind a pile of paint tins under Rory's house. But I can't get to it because someone's inside.

It could be someone after Roarer, it could be someone after me or it might be a random stranger. Rory's ex, Janet, has had the place made over. There's a strong smell of paint and there are no longer piles of rubbish in the backyard. I get around to where the path slopes down from the road and stand on my tippy-toes. In the bathroom a vase of flowers is sitting on the cistern and there's a tray of cosmetics by the door. I card the catch, ease up the bottom window sash and a hand-leap gets me inside, my right whiteside sending the flowers flying.

The vase shatters and the crash echoes through the house like cannon fire. In two strides I'm across the bathroom, my fist with the Luger in it thrust into the hall, but the opposition's faster. A sisal chop sends the gat flying and I feel my wrist gripped and someone starting to make barley twist out of my *radius* and *ulna* as my head comes into contact with the freshly painted jamb. The colour's off-white. I like off-white but not when it's wearing my blood. Something tells me I'm in trouble. It's not the astute agent.

Chapter 13

THE ASTUTE AGENT

I'm on one side of the door and he's on the other and my arm's in serious danger of breaking. At times like these, the brain works fast and my hypothalamus goes into overdrive. I run through the options. Top of the list is to die. After that comes breaking free by main force – impossible because his grip's too strong; following my arm into the hall – which is what he wants; or falling limp – the option of the obvious. The tray of cosmetics teeters on the edge of the bath as my knee hits it.

I feel searing pain as the pressure reaches tipping point. The elbow's the link between carriages and it takes up the slack as the train moves out of the station. The tray contains unguents, deodorants and astringents plus a lot of active constituents, most of them carrying the suffix: *DANGEROUS*. I grab the nearest canister with my free hand – fingers and thumb around the can, forefinger on the button – and launch myself through the doorway, turning *against* the arm twist, the pain of it blinding as I press the button and keep pressing. At first there's no reaction but just as my arm's about to give way, the hiss of escaping chemicals is joined by a scream as the active constituents find my assailant's eyes – a scream accompanied by a loosening of the grip and the return of my arm.

He's big which gives me part of the edge because the hall's narrow. He's also in pain which gives me the rest of the edge. I keep the spray aimed in the general direction of his face. While he's screaming, he's tearing at his eyes. The poet said, *Any man's death diminishes me.* This isn't death but it's the next best thing and I don't feel diminished by it. Instead I exult in his pain. He's on the floor trying to escape but I keep the spray aimed at him. *One day you'll go too far,* the shrink said. *You'll kill someone you don't intend to.* I take my finger off the trigger and he stops screaming.

I switch the can across to the bad hand, bend and shove the thug on his back with the other, while elbowing his hands from his face so I can see his features. He's youngish, his hair's trimmed to sandpaper and one tooth is capped with gold. Mullygrub ears, eyes that right now contain more blood than pupil and his clothing's smart casual. He doesn't stop me going through his pockets because he can't. There's nothing in them. I step back.

'What's your name?'

He can't see me and it's like he's lost his voice. It could be a ruse and people have been killed by ruses. He's wearing a fawn T-shirt with I HEART SYDNEY on it, gabardine daks and a nice pair of light-brown shoes – the clobber of choice if you want to get lost in the crowd. Big biceps and steel pectorals. Clearly he works out – although nothing's worked out for him today. I find my gat, bag it, drag Gold Tooth to his feet with my one good hand – contrary to what people think, a man on the ground has the edge on a man standing – and get him into the loungeroom, knocking over a lampstand on the way. I shake him till his teeth rattle.

'Who sent you?'

He sucks in his breath, borrowing time to get across the pain, at the same time lulling me towards a space where he can take me. I drop the can, drag down the curtains and use them to secure him to a chair. I go through his pockets a second time. He's smirking.

'You won't find nothin'.'

He's right, I don't. No more than an attitude that says he's a particular kind of thug belonging to a particular part of my life – but which part? He bears more than a passing resemblance to the corpses at the refuge. The cops found nothing on them either – a *nothing* that Monica said proved that the thugs were IRA. They could be triplets – the only difference being this one's still alive. I could beat him up but what would that prove? Only that the shrink was right and I'm a psychopath. So I desist, leaving the desirable residence in disarray and the thug tied to a chair.

I find Rube's box, tuck it under my arm and get away fast. There's nowhere else, so that's where I go.

'I thought you'd be back,' Mildred says. 'What is it this time – an ingrown toenail?'

'I need somewhere to stay.'

Mildred shrugs like she's seen it all before.

'Why not? Sure beats watching television.'

I look up Dr Sally Kane on the medical register, Gargle, the White Pages, everywhere I can think of but end up with a big fat zero so I ask Mildred to babysit Rube's box while I train it to Dashiell, Sally's hometown. It's the same country town with the same lazy shops and the same people wearing laughing-side boots and Akubras. I've rebadged myself – I'm wearing conservative dark-green daks, deep-brown velour jacket with a hunter's cut to it, a wide-brimmed Stetson in accordance with the mores of Dashiell, and whitesides – otherwise known as co-respondent's shoes, my usual footwear of choice. I'm packing a Pistolet Makarova – a gat with a long, heavy trigger pull to it but it'll have to do – as I make my way from the coach stop to the hospital known as Dashiell Basic.

I find a pumpkin at reception who's about as helpful as saltlick in a desert. Dr Kane might once have worked here, the pumpkin says, but she's here no longer. She might also once have lived at 48 Daisy Drive, Dashiell, but now she's nowhere.

'What do you mean *nowhere*? Brain surgeons don't just cease to exist.'

She doesn't say *this one did* but that's the subtext. 'Sorry but that information's privileged.'

'Why – because she's privileged and the rest of us aren't?'

The pumpkin reaches for the phone. 'I think you'd

better leave.'

Always check what they tell you, especially when the teller's a pumpkin. I find a fleet of Tonka toys in the driveway, mail in the letterbox addressed to someone else and the neighbours confirming that Sally Kane no longer resides at 48 Daisy Drive, Dashiell. The Royal Society for the Prevention of Cruelty to Surgeons has got no-one on their books called *Kane, Sally*, so after training it back to Sydney I find a computer café and roll back the flaps of time.

First stop: *Australia, Surgeons, Brain, Female* – but Sally's name isn't there, either. Second stop … Following the *Hood With No Hands* caper, a court case was scheduled and Sally would have been subpoenaed as a witness. It was a long time ago but courts, like the mills of God, grind slow. Because of who was involved – the Mafia – Sally would have been placed in a Witness Protection Program just like her husband. They're life-changers, WPPs. You can no longer be who you were or you'd be dead. The hood with no hands was Family, which means that an unfriendly witness – and Sally would be seen as unfriendly – would be marked out for the regulation bullet in the back of the head. Hank, the bartender at O'Leary's, the speakeasy, has got Rory's number.

'You only call when you need me,' Rory complains.

'When does anyone call anyone?' I cut to the

chase. 'I need an in to WPP, both here and in America.'

Rory parks his contrition. 'I got back in touch with The Dwarf when I was looking for work.'

The Dwarf's all of four-foot-eight, well over the mandatory height for dwarfs but still no giant. He was a big man in crime prevention before being found guilty of just about every crime in the book. Which means that he's a small man again – last seen acting as the rear-end of a horse in a circus. But he kept up his contacts – which makes him handy for Rory, who's a killer.

'And?'

'So, yeah, I can do that for you. What's it worth?'

It's an insecure line but now and then I've got to park the paranoia so I give him Sally 's name, adding, 'But there's no payment, Roarer – we're friends, remember?'

Roarer sighs. 'When do you want this?'

'The day before yesterday.' I remember the second reason for my call. 'Are you back with Janet?'

'Janet who?'

Chapter 14

DOWN AMONG THE TOMBSTONES

The parsonage is deserted but I find her near the cenotaph tending to the dahlias. When she looks up, the sun's in her hair and she looks like an angel. But she doesn't talk like one.

'What are you doing here?'

'I need information.'

Her hair's still red but her face is redder. Janet Q. Peters was never one of God's masterstrokes but now she's in serious need of a makeover.

'I'm not going back to Rory.'

I keep it smooth. 'Good decision, Janet. Roarer's a killer who'll never mend his ways. You did right to commit adultery with that preacher.'

She squints through her goggles. 'Are you having a go at me? Because if you are –'

I cut to the chase. 'When we met, you were working in a hospital in Dashiell and afterwards at the reception desk in an estate agent's. Where were you before that?'

'All over the place. My mother was a drifter.'

'Where did she drift to – specifically?'

'Northern NSW, Western Australia, Fiji – wherever her latest man led her.'

'Was she mixed up with magicians?' Her frown of incomprehension gives me the answer. 'Okay, next question: have you got it in for me?'

'Of course I've got it in for you! If it hadn't been for you I'd never have met that one-legged moron called Rory. Nor would I be trying to justify myself every second day to the preacher.'

'Is that all?'

'Isn't it enough?'

'Enough to kill me?'

Janet shakes her head. 'Being a pagan you wouldn't understand. As a Christian I follow the path of righteousness.' She fumbles the spade, drops it, bends to retrieve it. 'Which means that every day I struggle with the desperate urge to kill people.'

'What about adultery?'

Pandora's quick on her feet but Janet's slow. She brings her spade over her head like she's about to whack me. The bees buzz and the birds twitter. Only in my wildest dreams could she be Pandora. But I'm a detective, not a dreamer. I haul out the gat – an old Roth-Steyr with rotating barrel but it does the job.

'Don't kill me!' she cries. If she were Pandora she'd be behind a tombstone or at my throat. I park the gat and raise the fedora.

'You're not the woman I thought you were.'

'What's that supposed to mean?'

'Neither more nor less than it does.'

It's nice to be back at the ballet. It's Lisette Priée's swansong – she's danced *Swan Lake* for the last time and she's covered in feathers and curtseying her final curtsey on a stageful of flowers. She returns my eyebrow-raise and nods in the direction of the forecourt like we're performing a *pas de deux* before the *entr'acte*. She's a wild card but I've still got to play her.

'I've got a question for you, Lisette.' Except for the nice little tutu-clad body, the pixie face and the feathers, she's all ears; when we danced together, Lisette seemed to like me but it could have been just another performance. 'And my question is: what's your next act?'

'Being a proper parent, just like mine weren't.'

'I didn't know you had kids.'

She shrugs. 'How could you? We haven't seen each other since the death of the dancer.' In the *Bullets at the Ballet* caper a dancer got shot. 'You're not part of my life but if things had been different you might have been.'

She's lithe enough and the right age and she can act. 'Did you resent me for passing you up?'

'*I* was the one who passed *you* up, Rainbow.'

'Did you want to kill me?'

She adjusts her feathers; they're ruffled. 'You're a strange person but, no, I never wanted to kill you.'

'Did you want to follow me?'

'Ha, not likely.'

It'd be easy to check the detail, just like it'd be easy to find out if she's a mother. But I've learnt enough. She's not Pandora.

'Happy retirement,' I tell her.

'I'm not retiring. I'm taking up martial arts, it being a natural corollary to ballet.'

She's still not Pandora.

Next cab off the rank is my dead mate Harry's might-have-been-but-never-was squeeze, the dame who fed me a cock-and-bull story about Harry loving her and, after he died, leaving her a fortune. I find Babychino aka De Niece (or Denise) in Broadfoot Women's Reformatory, courtesy of an Identikit picture and someone who owed me a favour. She's wearing fetching Prussian-green coveralls like the rest of the inmates.

'Fancy meeting you here,' she says, all hard-faced candour. 'You always were a sucker for a pretty face and I had you fooled, didn't I?'

She's hard and she's fast and she could be Pandora except for her size and age – she's too young and too small. But instinct tells me to forget both. In my mind I replace the green outfit with black and put a knife in her hand. We're in a visitor's room with bars on the windows and I'm holding onto my strides because they took away my belt. Babychino's the original amoeba.

'How did you end up here, Denise?'

'That's not my real name but ultimately nothing's real – life's no more than a magician's trick. I had a scam going but the last jockstrap I tried it on turned out to be a copper.'

'What was the scam?'

'Getting suckers into hotel rooms on the promise of sex then hitting them over the head with a cosh and taking their money.'

'Subtle if not also highly original. How long have you been in the slammer?'

'Since the last time I saw you.' During which time Pandora paid me the odd visit, which means that Babychino's got the perfect alibi. 'Perhaps we could get together after I get out?'

She'd have to be Houdini to be Pandora. I tell her perhaps and clear out.

Next stop: Sally Kane.

Chapter 15

IN THE MUSEUM OF MODERN HEART

Nothing's secure if you know where to find it. According to the information obtained from The Dwarf, Sally Kane, brain surgeon, is still in Australia. Except there's been a change of name, address and occupation so now she's Sheila Keane, artist, presently living in the island state of Tasmania. After a great deal of to-ing and fro-ing, she finally agrees to see me.

I first came across Sally Kane in the case of the *Hood With No Hands*. She wanted kids but her husband didn't add up, so she hired me to do the maths on him. At least that's what she *said* she hired me for. She was a bona fide surgeon who knew her way around acting and psychiatry and she was beautiful and bright and, as a result of my investigation, she and her husband parted company. After which Sally and I also went our separate ways.

She's got to be Pandora.

There's still the stumbling block of age. She's older than Monica but all things being equal she's probably too young to be Pandora. But all things are never equal which means there's a chance I only *imagined* the early Pandora – with Sally picking up the reality where the chimera left off. It's a long shot but it might be the only shot I've got. I can't work out a motive but that can wait.

Her lips barely move as she glances nervously around and says, 'Are you sure you weren't followed?'

Her hair's black where it used to be blonde and she's wearing paint-spattered bib-and-tuck overalls with paintbrushes sticking out of the pocket plus a pair of sunglasses with wraparound frames. She's lost weight and she should be carrying a scalpel instead of a brush but I'd still recognise her – if not for the posture. She hasn't stopped glancing around since I arrived and I get the feeling that *I'm* not the one being followed.

I've taken the usual precautions. I flew to Adelaide under an assumed name – what other names are there? Then I caught a bus to Melbourne, wearing a change of clothing from Vinnies – brown daks, black coat with an orange fleck to it and a purple straw fedora. I spent the night in a doss house in Melbourne. Someone showed more interest in me than was good for either of us but I demobilised him and left. After which I ditched the hat, put on a grey wig and caught the ferry to Hobart. There was another joker on the boat but I shook him. Any other suspicious figures must have been in my imagination – ask the shrink. I envisage Sally wearing skin-tight black and armed with a knife. I'm wearing a roll-necked sweater, brothel creepers and cords and could pass for an artist myself.

'I'm always being followed, Dr Kane,' I tell her.

'Don't call me that. I'm Sheila Keane, I'm in fear for my life and I paint.'

'Why are you in fear for your life?'

She tells me what I know already and I check out the joint while she's doing so. We're in an art gallery that calls itself the Modern Art Derivative or MAD for short and the name fits like a tea cosy on the head of an idiot. A giant Meccano machine is clanking away in a corner, a square of black is titled *Preponderance of Virtues* and a naked dame's perched on a tea box. They favour words like *Live Art* and *Working Installations*. Sally Kane, brain surgeon – sorry, *Sheila Keane, artist* – chose the venue. The main light switch is to the left of the front door. I make with the conversation.

'When does your case come up?'

'I can't talk about it.'

Change of subject. 'Any of your stuff here?'

She waves her hand at what might be a self-portrait: an anguished face behind bars. There's no friendliness – in her gesture or in the portrait. 'We're not here to discuss art. Could you ask the questions you came here to ask and leave?'

'Okay. First question: going back to the *Hood With No Hands*, why did you employ me? You needed a gumshoe but why me when you could have hired anyone?'

'All those years ago I didn't tell you the truth.'

'From memory you rarely did.'

I position myself between him and Sally and speed up the questioning. 'You didn't pick me out of that paper by accident.'

She takes a deep breath. 'No, I – was already aware of you,' she answers softly; then because someone – an elderly woman – has moved in next to us, 'Isn't that a beautiful line?'

'Yours or that so-called painting's?' I shepherd her away from the gunman who's also looking for a line – a sightline. 'Don't fob me off with lines.'

'Being an artist it becomes a habit.'

We move and the man with the gun follows.

'So what's this other life you knew me from?'

'It was during my first posting as a neurosurgeon. I was called to an emergency – a man who'd been shot in the head. I removed the bullet and he lived for a few days but then he died. It was my first life-and-death operation and it was a failure. I was angry. I wanted to find the killer.'

I flip through my mental files, the ones preceding the *Rainbow* cases: twenty-something years of trial and error, error and trial – *The Body in the Basement*, *The Widow Who Wasn't*, *The Guatemalan and the Gun*, *The Mob Manifesto*, *The Die-Hard was a Dame*. I can't remember this particular death. 'And did you?'

'Did I what?'

'Track him down, find the gunman?'

We're out of the prank room and into another room too full of possibilities.

She nods. 'Yes, I did.'

Chapter 16

A SHOT IN THE DARK

'The victim was a crook,' Sally says, 'although his file didn't say it in so many words. While he was still alive, crooked types came to visit him, men in black coats who kept their hands in their pockets and didn't bring flowers. A cop told me a *gumshoe* shot him – that was the word he used, *gumshoe*. When I asked for a name he said there wasn't one. One day I called in sick.'

We're standing before a giant potato with six eyes called *Rebirth*. 'Doctors are natural detectives,' Sally goes on. 'We've got organised minds and are taught to classify and analyse. But the difference between us and people like you is that while doctors are dedicated to saving lives, people like you destroy them. I wanted to track down this man who put bullets in people's brains and I was prepared to put my job on the line to do it. It took me a month.'

'You're supposed to be a surgeon.'

'When *you* do it it's called detecting while I'm a meddler, is that it? I followed a trail of blood that led from a man with a bullet in his brain to a Sydney speakeasy with a heap of criminals in it. I came up with a name – Rainbow. But I still had to find you.'

'And you did that via the *Poisonal* columns. After which you stalked me.'

She shrugs. 'I was an actor, remember? I was never the same person twice. Sometimes I was an old woman, at other times I passed myself off as a man.'

'Did you carry a knife?'

'Are politicians liars? I'm a surgeon, remember.'

'Is that all you did? Follow me?'

'It was like stepping into a sewer. I didn't want to but I followed you. But after a while work claimed me back. I no longer had time.'

'Until you needed a private detective and remembered me. You wanted an excuse and your husband provided one so you rang up the number you'd found in the *Poisonals*.'

The first shot takes out the fake brain – the skull shatters and the synapses fade and so, too, do the main lights while the rest of the *installations* – that's what they call them: audio, visual, tactile, olfactory and probably tasty – must have been on a different circuit because they continue their *clackety-clacking*. The next shot merges with the background, ending up as no more than an echo in the overall assault on the senses, a natural extension of the whirring of electric motors, the rattle of old-fashioned destination signs and the hammer of waves on the rocks below: the report of a late-model .45 Canadian Para-Ordnance, the one with a stock made of cocobolo wood, a work of art that merges with the background like it belongs there.

The thin red line of a laser pierces the darkness, ending on the *sinister temporalis* of Sally's head like a tattoo telling a surgeon to *CUT HERE*. At such times there's no indecision. I grab her and we end up on the floor. Sally struggles to disentangle herself.

'They knew you'd lead them to me and that's what you've done!'

'Be quiet and keep your head down.'

Lasers possess a beginning as well as an end and I trace the beam to its source, making out a bearded face about where you'd expect one if it was attached to a thug holding a laser-mounted equaliser. It's a high-risk shot because there are too many people about so I hold my fire as I rib-crawl my way to the door. The main switch is to the left. I flick it and light floods the room. The gunman's searching for Sally and I just get a bead on him when someone shouts, 'Is there a doctor in the house?'

Nuns give themselves to Christ, cops swear allegiance to law and order and medicos vow to save lives. Sally identifies herself – however much she pretends to the contrary she's still a doctor. I grab her again, another shot whangs over her head and by the time I look up, Laser Man's gone. My first thought is that he's Pandora and after me; the second, more accurate, diagnosis is that he's a Mafia hitman after Sally. Which makes him a two-edged sword and anyone could lose their head on the backswing. I scramble up but I'm too late. I turn back to Sally. 'We're leaving.'

But she's tending to the injured; she shoulders me

away. 'No – *you're* leaving! Go away from me as far as you can and never come back!' Her voice turns suddenly tender. 'Don't move, darling.'

The last words aren't directed at me.

You see a shadow behind the installations, so you go after it. Only to find when you get there that it's gone. I hurtle through the gallery, gat at the ready, but it's like they create this stuff to hide killers. The gunman's gone but not forgotten because you never forget a gunman. This one was short, bearded and black-coated. But next time the beard will have gone and he'll be wearing something different. The sirens become ambulances, fire engines and cops as I hurdle a bunch of empty beer cartons. Or maybe they're works of art.

Her address is in the White Pages – *Sheila Keane, Artist, So-and-so Street, So-and-so suburb, Hobart*; her home's a converted barn; and I find the documents under a flea-bitten couch with a paint-splattered sheet over it. The papers confirm that she's a surgeon with a certificate in acting from NIDA and a degree in psychiatry. But the appended list of operations doesn't include a man with a bullet in his brain. I return the papers to their hidey-hole. Sally's career is shot to pieces but she still wants to stay alive which is why she made up the story about the bullet. At least that's a reason I can accept. Someone's arrived outside; I make myself scarce.

Someone who knew me and Sally were linked

followed me and now I've left her exposed – tending to the victims of a shooting. There are two reasons to return to the gullery:

1. Sally could be Pandora and
2. I don't want to be responsible for her death.

I'm greeted by what they call in the classics a *scene of chaos* – meaning cars all over the place. Relatives and friends have arrived, along with TV vans, investors worried about their investments, artists wringing their hands over the fate of humankind plus the usual ambulances, cop cars and fire engines. And maybe also the killer.

I never trusted Sally and now I trust her even less but I got her into this mess and now I've got to get her out of it. A cop confronts me but he's overworked and under-brained so he lets me past. I count two bodies along with another one that could end up that way. Sally's arguing with a fat man waving a stethoscope.

'This is a small town on a small island,' the fat man's saying, 'where everyone knows everyone else. I'm a doctor who's also an art lover and you're Sheila Keane, artist. You're not a doctor so you can't tend to the sick and injured.'

Sally's caught between her oath and a hard place. 'People are dying, as in *sharp nose, hollow eyes, collapsed temples, ears cold, contracted and with their lobes turned out, skin about the face rough, distended and parched, colour greenish or dusky.*' She glares at the fat man. 'If I wasn't a doctor, how would I know the Hippocratic *facies*?'

'I don't know what you're talking about. Officer!'

I move in and flash a badge. Any badge. They

She shrugs. 'I could have dealt with my husband myself. But I had an ulterior motive.' She looks around and I look around with her; we're surrounded by more body parts than you'd find in a mass murderer's freezer. 'Why am I telling you this?'

'Because you want me out of your hair but you also know I'm not leaving until I've got some answers and the longer I'm around the greater the likelihood someone will draw conclusions. A series of unfortunate events led you here and you don't want them to lead any further. You've either appeared in court or you've yet to give evidence. Either way you're afraid for your life and you want to be shot of me.'

Her face clears and for the first time this session – despite the hair, the overalls, the paintbrushes and the hunched shoulders – I see again the beautiful Sally. 'It's nothing personal,' she murmurs. 'I was grateful for your help but unfortunately it led to –' she shrugs '– this. And you're right – I don't want things to get any worse than they already are.'

I take a deep breath and it's full of inevitability. 'I'll leave after you answer my questions.' I glance around; she's got me doing it now. 'Why did you hire *me*?'

'Because I saw your ad in the newspaper.'

'A lot of gumshoes advertise.'

'Your ad was in the *Personals* and I was looking in the *Personals*.'

'Some people call them *Poisonals*.' I glance around again and that's when I notice him: he's wearing a black three-quarter length coat and a beard and he's carrying a gun held lengthwise under his coat.

never look. 'Inspector Moriarty at your service,' I say. 'What's the problem?'

Chapter 17

SISTER PSYCHOLOGY

The fat man waves his stethoscope. 'This woman's a fraud, spouting nonsense about *faeces* while pretending to be a doctor when she quite clearly isn't.'

'Thank you.' I grab hold of Sally's arm. 'I'll take it from here. Come with me, ma'am.'

I shepherd her past bodies with real doctors tending to them, real policemen not blocking my way because I'm just another cop doing his job and the job's hard enough without having to deal with fools.

'Let me go!' she says.

'The gunman could come back,' I tell her. I nod to a constable. 'I'm Australian Federal Police. I found this woman posing as a doctor and I'm taking her in for questioning. As if we haven't got enough on our plate without charlatans.'

She's still struggling. 'I swore an oath to save people and I'm going to save them if it kills me!'

I shake my head as I usher her outside. 'Right now you've only got one job and that's to stay alive. Do you have your driver's licence with you?'

'I drove here, so, yes.' I get her behind the wheel of her car; a battered VW; she starts it then pauses. 'This means we're going back to the mainland, doesn't it? That's why I need the licence – not just to drive but in case they ask for my ID.' She thinks some more. 'If I ask questions, you'll only lie. It's like a doctor asking a patient if their appendix needs operating on when it's really their leg. I realise you have to take me because my cover's blown but first I have to collect some clothes.'

I shake my head again or the road's shaking it for me. 'If you go home all you'll collect is a bullet. They're waiting for you. These people want you dead.'

She nods.

'Where are we going?'

'To the bus terminal and from there to Adelaide.'

She nods again. 'That means the airport and Sydney.'

We dump the car and cab it the rest of the way. I call Roarer and tell him we're coming.

Back in Sydney, Roarer drives us to the caravan belonging to Sue Mahoney – Tsunami – the one that's hidden in the bush off the Bratwurst Parkway. Tsunami's missing, presumed dead, so she's unlikely to have any further use for it.

'This is your home for a while,' I tell Sally.

'How long's *a while*?'

'As long as you want to stay alive or until they

work out where you are – whichever comes first. The stove works, there's food in the cupboard and the cutlery's in the drawer under the sink.'

The key to the caravan was on the tyre but that's not the key I'm after. It's been staring me in the face ever since I started interviewing the dames. Janet Q. Peters' father figures; Lisette Priée with her talk of parenting; Denise's father fixation; my own haphazard relationship with Imogene. Back at Mildred's I go through Aunt Rube's files again. The heading on the one I want reads: *THE COMING OF RAINBOW.*

It was a shock to the system. Here I was, a middle-aged private investigator, a bachelor girl from way back, suddenly lumped with a kid. Not a lifestyle choice I'd put up my hand for but what else could I do? My brother's a bastard and the kid's probably one, too … There's more of the same – Aunt Rube's as eloquent on paper as she was in life. I was five and can't recall much of what happened but Rube revivifies it – the trip from Nimbin in the Kombi with my father and his latest blonde; me half-stunned because my mother and sister had just gone up in flames before my eyes; while the grieving widower – a word that at age five I didn't even know – was acting like he'd swatted a fly; arriving in Sydney, the first home outside a hut that I'd known; and my father telling me to bugger off.

What does it eat? One thing I do know – the father

won't be back, not in my lifetime. At least he gave me a last-resort address …

The files are ordered, annotated and indexed, complete with cross-references. It takes all of my narrative detecting skills – the application of search theory Rube taught me, as in: use a logical approach, be bold, use the grey matter, persevere. Thanks to my acrobatics in the gullery back in Hobart, my left arm's pretty well useless and it'll be a while before it's fully operative again. The light in the Hobbit hovel's penumbra and Aunt Rube's files are spread out before me on Mildred's rust-sprung couch.

There's nothing in the diary so I switch to the case files going back fifty years. I give each batch of papers a good shake but no handy scrap falls out. I turn to the file labelled *CONTACTS*, the one I've been avoiding because I haven't got a name. I know that even from the grave, Rube won't make it easy for anyone rummaging through her affairs. Any names and addresses will be for my eyes only, which means they'll be in code.

Somewhere in the 1980s the coded contact details are joined by email addresses. Criminals rub shoulders with police commissioners, spies with terrorists, politicians with spivs. A lot of the time it's hard to tell the difference. Reinvented names are accompanied by tags consisting of two, three, four or five letters. I cast my mind back. *You must have at least one language in reserve,* Rube drummed into me

– a language confined to a restricted group of people. There'll be times when you'll need it. This is one of those times.

Rube had a great many codes but I dispense with the ones where numbers are substituted for letters or the alphabet's inverted because they're far too simple for this exercise. She used French, Latin and Greek derivatives; Morse code; algebraic symbols; and complex combinations thereof. I'm still trying to find a name and address when Mildred returns. She reminds me of Rube.

'You need a wife,' she says, bustling about. 'Fancy a grown man like you getting about on your own. Dinner's tofu curry – vegan, which I believe is to your liking. A lifetime in hospitals has taught me how bad food can be. Would you select a wine? What are you up to?'

When I get to my feet I'm suffering near-paralysis from vein clamp and can smell the sweet-scented mixture of turmeric, apple blossom and garlic. I uncork a Corbiere *vin de table* as Mildred repeats her last question and I let the genie out of the bottle.

'I'm looking for my father.'

Night's fallen and Sister Mildred should open a restaurant.

'Nursing's not all badinage and bandages,' she says. 'To a great extent, recovery depends on Sister Psychology. And Sister Psychology tells me you're in trouble – you've told me little or nothing, much like my daughter.'

We go on eating in silence – if that's the right word when there's a continuous roar of traffic outside, low-flying planes rattling the roof tiles and a pack of wildcats loose in my brain. Rube numbered her codes from one to fifty and the relevant code could be any one of them. *You've told me little or nothing,* Mildred said. It's the same with the address file.

Mildred continues, 'Nurses get used to talking to themselves. I tended to wounded soldiers from Vietnam, old men with hip replacements and women with the kind of complaints that women get. And Sister Psychology worked every time. What worries most patients isn't what you say – it's what you *avoid* saying.'

'I thought *patients* were called *guests* now.'

She sips her wine. 'Yes, and don't those code words make everyone feel so much *better*? Modern hospitals think meaningless phrases are cure-alls. That it's not *what* you say but *how* you say it – which is usually the opposite of what is. All you need is to find a euphemism and you've found the cure. As if someone on the point of dying can be healed by words.'

Chapter 18

THE MAN FROM LOTTO

All you need is to find a euphemism and you've found the cure. It's like the Rosetta Stone unlocking the mysteries of Egypt. I've got to work out what the words mean on the surface then set the hieroglyphics beside them and track down their opposites. While Mildred clears away the plates I recheck the relevant ciphers: *Gentle Violence* which several codes along the track becomes *Gentian Violet*. Which transposes into *Prater Violet* which becomes – I recheck the code – *Peter Violente*.

Now for the address. *The Dark One*, plus a street name and number, also in code. By a process of elimination, the suburb becomes the obverse of what it appears – *you see what you want to see –* just like Mildred said. That means *Dark* becomes any one of *Light, Clear, Unshaded, Illuminated* or multiples thereof. Followed by *One* then the seemingly misspelt *Minuse* – when Rube never misspelt anything. Which makes it *One Minus-e.* Which could be anything but includes the very real possibility of *Brighton, Melbourne.* Using Mildred's computer I log into Gargle Earth and enter the suburb, street name and number my father gave Rube and Rube subjected to her elaborate code.

At Tullamarine Airport I buy a ticket for the big red bus plus a travel card. At Southern Cross station I switch to a blue and silver train that's *not* going to Brighton and after that catch a train that is. I get out where the railway intersects Bay Street, head north, switch to a side street, then swing east. Big houses, high walls, lots of ivy – just the place if you want to hide and the cops are subservient. I'm unarmed because they don't let you take gats on planes, which is no bad thing if you're psychotic.

Weeds poke through the fence and signs say *NO ENTRY*. Number 53 Cornucopia's begging to be put out of its misery, the U-lock on the gate's an easy pick and the path's heaped with snail-chewed mail. I imagine what it looked like when my father arrived forty years ago. The house would have had the sparkle of new paint, the weatherboards wouldn't have broken away, tiles wouldn't have slipped off the roof and the weeds would have been lawn. And my father would have had the sparkle of adventure in him – he was in his thirties, his wife was dead and he had a new dame on his arm. A dog barks, something slithers under the house and I go in.

Dust and desuetude, darkness and death. My checks showed the joint's owned by someone called Gambetta. A yellowed letter says the water and power were disconnected years ago and

never reconnected. No-one's lived here for ages
– Gambetta being too old, too rich or both. The
mould in the fridge is hardcore and the floor's pulp.
I start at the back of the house because you've got to
start somewhere.

I would have missed it except I was looking, treading
on the lines of nails indicating the position of the
bearers because the floorboards were unsafe. A flock
mattress lies in a corner, a cheap earring lies next to
the mattress and a faded photo of the Delhi Banana
hangs askew on the rose-print wall. I get splinters
under my nails digging the thing out from behind
the skirting – time and the elements have worked on
it like they have on the mail. I brush it clean, pocket
it and move on.

I've got none of my tools of trade apart from
intuition but that'll have to do. The wallpaper in
the front room, east, is Laura Ashley, circa 1980.
My father would have arrived here in 1974, before
the wallpaper. I peel it away where mould has
begun the work for me to find more of what I'm
after. Above the phone jack in the hall are names,
phone numbers, addresses and squiggles, as well
as a lot of cryptic messages and lazy thoughts
that would have made sense at the time but make
little now: *Protest makes perfect*; *When the mouse
is away, the cat sleeps*; *Ice Queen*; a heart with
P.V. arrow A.G. on it – heavily pencilled like
the person who did it was under the influence of

something, call it delusion. I'm used to it now –
it's my father's handwriting.

It takes me a day – a day in which seconds turn into
minutes and minutes into hours. I find a public
telephone and punch in the numbers only to come
up with nothing because, over time, phone numbers
change. It's easy to find the addresses that once
belonged to the numbers but they turn into stone
walls. All bar one: 7 Lucretia Avenue, Ophelia. A
late-model Jaguar's sitting in the driveway and an
old maid opens the door.

'I'm from Lotto, the government gambling
institution you can trust. I need residents' names.'

The old maid peers at me with suspicion while
restraining a cross Alsatian-mastiff. A *very* cross
Alsatian-mastiff. 'What do you want?'

'If I knew what I wanted I wouldn't be here. How
long have you been in residence?'

Pride overcomes suspicion. 'I'm an old family
retainer – forty-one-and-a-half years.'

'Who else lives here? Starting with the name
and occupation of the head of the house, like in a
census.'

The maid's going to get into trouble whichever
way she bounces; somewhere behind her a baby's
crying and somewhere else a newsreader's saying
there's been another earthquake in Nepal. The maid
takes the line of least resistance; she wants to hear
the news or settle the baby, most likely both. But

before she can do anything she's got to answer the question.

'Dr Jonathan Gambetta, Queen's Counsel – the Victorian Government changed back from *Senior* Counsel because people like Dr Gambetta complained – is in his chambers and Mrs Gambetta's having her hair done.'

The maid starts to close the door but I put my foot in it.

'Would that be *Gambitta* with an *i*?'

'No, with an *e*. And a double-*t*.'

The baby's wails have increased in intensity, the news goes into overdrive and to add to the maid's anxiety a jug's boiling over. Old mansion, ancient jug.

'Are we talking about the same person? What are Dr Gambetta's antecedents?' I take it slow – it makes them jittery and keener to talk to get rid of this unwanted intrusion so they can deal with the primary source of their anxiety. 'Mother, father, grandparents, uncles, aunts.'

'I only know the name of Dr Gambetta's maiden aunt – Annita. And, yes, she lived here.'

'Age?'

'She's dead.'

'What age would she have been, had she lived?'

'I don't know – sixty? No, wait a minute, I know exactly – sixty-one.'

'What did she die of?'

'A broken heart. Look, I'm busy, would you please leave?'

The initial's right, the age is in the ballpark and so is the broken heart. I please leave.

She remembers something as she closes the door.
'Does Dr Gambetta get the prize?'
'I'll come back,' I tell her.
And I do.

Chapter 19

A ROLAND FOR AN OLIVER

I've changed into a snug-fitting black tracksuit courtesy of Vinnies and I'm carrying a torch but I don't know exactly what I'm looking for. As a precaution I sedate the dog, disable the alarm and climb in through the pantry window of Number 7 Lucretia Avenue. I learnt as much as I could on my first visit. What I'm looking for now could be in the study, which should be on the ground floor, well away from the nursery. Which, going by the screams I heard earlier, is off to the right. I go through the pointers that say this is the right place:

1. My father had a low female-attention span and was sick of his blonde
2. The initials of the blonde's successor were *A.G.*
3. One of the phone numbers, adjusted for time, matches this address
4. A resident was one Annita Gambetta – right initials
5. Calculating back from age sixty-one, in 1978 Annita Gambetta would have been twenty-one – which for my cradle-snatching father was pretty much the right age.

The study's not on the ground floor, the stairs squeak and the floorboards in the hallway upstairs are bare. I've put the pooch in dreamland for twenty minutes, which means I've got fifteen minutes before it starts calling in its IOUs. I switch off the torch as I move past a roomful of snores. The baby's whimpering and the study's at the end of the hall.

I ease the door shut and turn on the light. The walls are covered with books, complete with designer footstool to reach the upper echelon; while in the middle of the room is a desk containing a gilt-framed photograph of a man in a wig who must be Gambetta, a green telephone and a silver letter opener. There's the usual array of fine chairs and an ancient-looking book in a display case by the window.

I already know that my father was – is – not a nice person. Aside from dumping me, he hived off with a blonde the moment Mum dissed herself. Everything points to his soon thereafter abandoning his blonde for a dame with the initials A.G. Working forward, one Annita Gambetta had an affair, relationship, *connection* with my father while her nephew – whose study this is – was a kid. My dad was an opportunist. What I want is here somewhere.

Going by the instructions on the packet containing the sedative I fed the pooch I've got thirteen minutes left and valuable time is always saved by analysis. Good lawyers – and going by the signs, Gambetta's good – leave little to chance. If there's anything of significance, it won't be sitting up on the desk with a smile on its face saying *Take me.* The prints on the wall are of things legal and for show while what I'm looking for is quasi-legal and private. Official documents would be in his chambers but I'm not looking for official documents. I'm after unofficial ones.

If there's a safe in his chambers – and there would be – a safe here would be an unnecessary duplication. What I'm looking for doesn't have to be all that secure – just away from the prying eyes of a maid. The desk drawers are locked but it would be *logical* not to keep anything of value in the desk. Any one of these 5000 tomes might be fake, with the words Blackstone's *Law of Torts* on the outside and pornography within. But that would be too obvious. So where is it? Anything hidden would be personal – love letters, children's drawings, the odd obscene postcard. I calculate the size of such a collection and come up with a bundle slightly smaller than the quarto-sized book in the display case.

The volume is Foxxe's *Book of Martyrs* and it's open like a pair of innocent hands. The cabinet's a fish tank minus water, its lid locked but not secure. I ease it open with the letter opener. Gambetta's got little sentiment – he's a lawyer, after all – and although the book's a rarity it's been gutted. What I'm looking for is in the left side cut-out.

I could take it all but I don't need it all. I only need what's mine, my inheritance – the letter with the name and address on it. The faint odour of women's perfume wafts from a scrap of tear-wrinkled paper; a sepia photograph of a woman in a bikini smiles for the dickey-bird; a child's drawing reveals a liking for elephants; there's an interesting document signed by a well-known criminal, deceased; and a one-page note in a hand I recognise – addressed and dated. I check my watch. Five minutes to go. The dog growls. So much for the promise on the packet. I pocket the note, replace the book, close the cabinet and straighten to find Gambetta in the doorway, holding a gun.

'I could shoot to kill,' he says. 'However, were I successful I could be deemed to have used *undue force* as defined in *obiter dicta* in judgments on trespass. I could shoot to wound only I might miss. I find myself caught between Scylla and Charybdis, a rock and a hard place. Either way' – here he waves the gun, a pretty Steyr M40 automatic with triangular sights – 'I imagine you'd prefer this little chap not to go off, particularly with you at the pointy end of it.'

In wig and gown in a courtroom and waving a sheaf of papers, Gambetta could be impressive. But with his hair all over the place, wearing a loose-tied paisley dressing gown and waving a gun, he looks and sounds like any other two-bit criminal – of unsound mind and dangerous.

'I must be in the wrong house.'

He advances on the desk with the phone on it. 'Yes, you must, mustn't you?' He waves the gun even more. 'Stand back.'

I stand back, he picks up the handpiece and I make like I just thought of something. 'But just in case I'm in the right house, I'm here on behalf of *Peter Violente*, who I believe is an old friend of yours – or at least of your aunt.'

He drops the phone like it's hot. He's big and well-built but I could take him, even with the gun, because he's off-guard. But I don't have to. I've got his attention, which is what I'm after.

'I beg your pardon?'

'It was a matter of blackmail and settlement – I expect you'd regard it as a contract.'

'You're not making sense,' he says.

I translate it into legalese. 'Although the two principals on your side are dead, it still looks bad. Bad enough to lose you your membership of the Melbourne Club – I believe they're still particular about such matters.' It makes me no better than my father but he didn't have a gun at his head. 'Your father did something illegal and my father found out about it, via pillow talk with your aunt. The contract showing payment by your father to mine is tantamount to an admission of guilt.'

'What do you want?'

'My father's most recent address.'

The dog's growling; next thing the baby will start crying; followed shortly thereafter by the appearance of a wife or the maid.

Gambetta's eyes flicker to the door. 'Is that all you want?'

'That's all.'

The lawyer considers his response, weighs it against the alternatives and decides in the only way he was ever going to. 'Your father was in touch with me only recently – after even more money. I'll tell you where he is if you return what you stole from me and inform him I'm not paying any more.'

When I reach into my pocket, he flinches; I'm a burglar, after all, as well as the son of a blackmailer and clearly no slouch in that department myself. 'Don't worry, I'm not armed.' I place the note on his desk. 'Now you can either tell me where he is or shoot me; I strongly recommend the first option.'

'His last-known address was Hamilton Street, Prahran, in Melbourne – number seventy, I think.' Gambetta pockets the paper. 'It's a men's refuge as far as I know. Which would mean that he'd fallen about as low as he could go when he last demanded money, which wasn't so many months ago.' He flicks the gun like he's seen it done on television. 'And in my book that's *quid pro quo* – which is Latin for, *It's all you're going to get in exchange for that piece of paper.* In other words, *a Roland for an Oliver.* You have nothing in writing and I haven't written a cheque so this didn't happen – it's just momentarily embarrassing.' He levels the gat. 'Now if you'll fulfil your undertaking and leave, I'll fulfil mine and not shoot you.'

Chapter 20

THE MYXO MAN

Skid row's skid row, whether it's in New York, Paris, London or Melbourne. It's no particular street in no particular part of town, more an attitude – a figure under a blanket, a shape in a doorway, a wraith, usually with its hand out. I'm my father's son and should want what's best for him. But looking at the figure before me I feel nothing.

I never really knew him. There was a young man who abandoned a small boy but memories need reinforcements and I didn't even have any photos. He could have been short, tall, fat, thin, handsome or plug-ugly and anything might have happened since. The old man shuffling along Chapel Street has feet that are blackened and scraggy hair and his crumple-legged, shiny-bummed pants are held up with twine. If it's my father he's not just my past, he's also my future.

He goes to cross the road but a tram dings its warning bell, causing him to stumble back onto the kerb. To attract all those women he must have had something. But that would have been no more than ersatz, bravado and charm. Because he would also have been fearful – fearful of what he'd done to my mother, fearful of losing what little there was left to him, fearful of what was to come. If I'm paranoid, this is where I got it.

When the old man's eyes wander my way, I see myself – the same mashed-in features, the same nose, same chin. When he finally notices me, he assumes I'm a mugger or a cop and veers away. I'm no more than a corpse's length from him. Close enough to smell the stench, close enough to not want to be here. *You're too close,* Monica Best warned. When I was a kid on the funny farm, I chased rabbits with myxomatosis – the disease that makes their eyes bulge and eventually kills them. That's what I'm following now – a sick animal staggering towards death. I feel myself recoil, wanting to get away. Then I touch the objects in my pocket. Apart from which, there was the writing on the wall.

It was stupid chasing those rabbits – even as a kid I knew that. They were good for nothing because they were diseased. When you caught one, what did you do with it? I stare at the figure before me. Can he think, talk and perform the functions necessary for survival? I don't want to be anywhere near him. I let him draw away. *You're too close,* Monica warned.

I turn and when I look back he's gone. The sun's a burning ember in a grey sky and there's an alternative. I could forget Pandora, forge a new life for myself and let my father rot in the sun. Then I hear my mother shrieking as she went to her death, together with my sister Sophie. And Pandora. That's when I remember what I'm here for and what I've got to do.

I break into a run. A boy on a bike passes, a woman smiles, leaves flutter from the trees. When I reach the corner of Watson and Chapel I still can't see him – there's too many shoppers, too much traffic. He's got away. I found my father only to lose him again.

Then I make out the figure on the bridge and hurry towards it before I lose him forever. When I grab his arm, it's a matchstick and the stench coming from him is overpowering. He tries to pull away but he's too weak. He's smaller than I thought and the whites of his eyes are yellow. I've made a mistake.

'Leave me alone, you bastard, or I'll …'

It's an empty threat, a parrot's curse. He's been on life's receiving end for too long and there's no strength left in him. This can't be my old man. Whoever it is has decided I'm a cop.

'What law am I breaking, tell me that! Can't a man be left alone? Who do you think you are?'

'I'm your son.'

The wretch cackles. 'Which son? Jesus, there are hundreds of them.' He rubs his head. 'That's what they always said about me – that Lothario's got kids all over the place.'

I followed the directions Gambetta gave me, a social worker at the hostel directed me to the old man's haunts and after a day searching the streets of Melbourne I've come up with this. Only to find that I'm most likely wrong. In my desperation to find my father I forgot to be a detective. The thing before me is what I *feared* my father had become, I'm seeing what I *expected* to see, twisting this old man to fit some childish image from an Identikit. I need proof.

'You're not Lothario, you're *Violente* – Peter Violente.' I can't say more, mustn't muddy the water; what I need is further confirmation apart from the smell – proof positive that this is my father. His eyes go dead, his body sags and I grab him before he falls. 'Who are you?'

'I told you – I'm Lothario.'

It can't be him because I can't bear it to be him. My father's a strutting dandy waving an ebony cane with a silver handle on it, a rich widow by his side – healthy, strong and in charge of his life.

'Does the name Annita Gambetta ring a bell?'

He pulls away, trying to free himself. 'Who are you?'

'I already told you – I'm your son.'

'I haven't got a son.'

'But you just said –'

He peers out of the fug, his watery eyes hooded. 'Who did you say you were?'

'The name's Rainbow.'

He shakes his head. 'What kind of name's *that*?'

I let go his matchstick arm and turn away. It was a futile exercise, a wild goose chase, a madman's impulse. *You're too close*, Monica had warned. While the shrink said, *You need treatment before you kill someone.* A tram rattles past, the racket rearranging the old man's words until they're no more than an echo.

'*My little Rainbow!*' It's the voice of my mother. '*He's so pretty, this little son of ours. Oh, we must have another and another …*' The parrot's mimicry ceases, to be replaced by a harsher voice, the voice of reality.

'There was only one choice and I took it.'

I can't believe it's him. In some dingy dive this derelict overheard my real father say those words and he's imitating him. He's of unsound mind and doesn't know what he's saying. One last try.

'I want one-word responses.' If he's who I need him to be, he would have gone through the routine many times. 'You've played the one-word game?' He nods, interested despite himself. 'All right, I want the first word that comes into your head. *Children.*'

'Burden.'

'Wife.'

'Victim.'

'Blame.'

'Sex.'

'Home.'

'Nimbin.'

'Pandora.'

The old man's eyes hood even more and he shakes his head – to clear it but also because he doesn't want to acknowledge that he knows the name. 'There were a lot of women in my life but I don't remember anyone called Pandora.'

I haven't got all I want but you never get all you want. Get all you want and you stop looking.

'Why did you say *Nimbin*?'

The guarded look returns. 'It was just a game. Life's a game.'

'Don't take refuge in stupidity.'

'What else is there to take refuge in?'

It's what I'd say; it must be him; I take his arm. 'You're coming with me.'

'That's what you think.'

This time I hang on. 'No, old man, it's what I *know*.'

At Tullamarine airport the dame in the cobalt-blue uniform has other ideas. 'I'm sorry but we can't take him.'

I've arranged for Roarer to pick us up at Mascot and through a Melbourne contact of Ace Mollema's I've obtained IDs for me and the old man that say we can drive. A gold driver's licence for me and a silver one for the old man. *We're Sammy and Bert Smith, father and son – I'm Bert and this is Sammy.* At the Salvos I got him a pair of sky-blue daks, an orange shirt and a pair of sneakers to cover the feet but he's still got the beard, he still stinks and the dame in the uniform comes around the counter and draws me aside.

'I'm sorry, sir, but we have strict regulations. There are other customers to consider and we'd get complaints.' The old man's too close to her; she edges away. 'Dementias can cause havoc.'

'He's not a dementia.'

'Then what's wrong with him?'

'His wife died.' It's not a lie. 'I've got to get him to Sydney.'

'Can't you go by train?'

'The train's too slow.'

The airline dame considers her options and realises she hasn't got any. She takes one of those breaths without any options in it.

'Do you have any baggage?'
'Only my dad.'

Chapter 21

NO TIME FOR MOURNING

After we touch down I park the old man with Roarer. They're two of a kind, last seen heading towards the Cross in an iridescent-pink Shangri-la coupé discussing the cross merits of dames. I cab it to the caravan off the Bratwurst Parkway, hand the cabbie a C-note and tell him to wait. Sally opens the door. She doesn't invite me in. I come straight to the point.

'We're going on a little journey.'

Her colouration indicates a state of excitement which would impede coherent thought. 'I'm not going anywhere except away from here. I'll contact the witness protection people and tell them I want out of their stupid program. Anything's better than a life on the run. I'll go back to medicine. Those thugs won't dare touch me.'

I hitch the gat. 'Have you got a preferred funeral parlour? I'll be happy to make all necessary arrangements.'

She considers me while the alizarin crimson in her cheeks fades to pink; even angry, she's beautiful. 'I really don't like you, Rainbow,' she says at last.

'Where are we going?'

'You'll know when we arrive. In the meantime I'm taking you to town where you'll buy three autumn-coloured tracksuits – sizes big, medium and small; black leotards and tights for night-time wear for yourself; a first-aid kit; torches; and backpacks for three. Plus a pair of binoculars. Oh, and some stuff from a theatrical supply shop that turns hair white.' I hand her a wad of dough. 'That should cover it. We'll meet under the clock at Central.'

'Is that all?'

I repocket my wallet. 'No, it's just the beginning.'

She's no longer Hélène Dalmatian. Instead she's Helena Dannazione, a barista in an eatery called Discord in Concord. I ease my way past too many black shirts, white suspender braces and hard looks and at first she doesn't recognise me. Memories belong to contexts and when she last saw me I was bald and we were in France. Change the context and you forget who was in it.

'Rainbow!' she says finally. 'Hang on, that should be – what should it be?'

'Arthur Halliwell. When you last saw me I was a bald accountant.' There are a few familiar faces but there are always familiar faces – what's important are the unfamiliar ones. 'But Rainbow will do. Got a minute?'

'I guess so.' A figure looms behind her and I slip my fist under my jacket; this would be Sugar

Daddy No. 3 or maybe it's No. 9 and he might be dangerous; she changes her mind. 'I mean, no, I haven't got a minute, I'm busy. Coffee?'

'Three shots and black like my conscience.' A few years back she was a waltz in the moonlight, an unnecessary evil who became a necessary one. Her watch waggles on her wrist as she taps the used coffee grounds from the ladle and replaces them with fresh ones. Meanwhile the figure behind her drifts away; the one I've got to watch is the one by the door. 'I need some information.'

'I know nothing you need to know.'

'You knew me before you knew me, didn't you?'

'That doesn't make sense.'

'Nothing and nobody makes sense. Were you ordered to come into my life or did you happen upon it by accident?'

Her lips tighten but she's still got those beautiful eyes – amethyst-coloured, the shape of sloes, berries to die for, like I nearly died for her. She yanks her hand away from the machine. It might be guilt or it might be the steam.

'It was an accident,' she says.

'What – coming into my life or burning your hand?'

'Both.'

'Lie and I'll stay, Dannazione. But tell me the truth and I'll leave.'

She lowers her voice. 'And when you do, will you promise to stay away?'

The figure by the door is moving towards us, hand in pocket – evil is as evil does and it's a living. I flick the safety to *Off* as I turn back to the dame.

'Answer the question – were you in my life before you were in it? Did you know me before I knew you? Were you tailing me?'

'All right, yes!' She's hissing like the coffee machine now. 'Someone told me to follow you.' It must have been Arthur Flax, her then sugar daddy, who was hand-in-glove with a bunch of crooks but is now dead. 'I know what you're thinking but it wasn't Arthur. It was –'

Silencers make a sound like a coffee machine and that's what this one's like – helium escaping from a balloon, a puff of breath, the hiss of a snake. As Dannazione slides to the floor, she's got what she wants – she'll never see me again and this particular sugar daddy will be her last. The figure who was by the door has nearly reached us while several other gats are also aimed in our direction, most of them made in Italy.

When I hit the floor, my gun barrel's smoking and Hell and Damnation – born Hélène Dalmatian but rebadged as Helena Dannazione – is staring sightless at me under the counter. There's no time for mourning. I snake-belly my way to the back door, through the *cucina*, into the *gabinetto* and out into the lane, accompanied by the usual fusillade. Not all the gats are muffled and some are cannons. Dannazione might be dead but she's still in the *PANDORA PENDING* file as I upset the wheelie bins. When there are guns after you, always upset the wheelie bins.

Gertrude Match looks innocent but she always looked innocent – a lightweight beauty with a heavyweight smile. But innocent or guilty I don't want her dead. Which is why I covered my tracks after leaving the death caff and why I don't hang around now. I put the question to the background of Madame Blavatsky banging out the fairy dance from the *Nutcracker* like a Death March while little feet shuffle on the bare wooden floorboards of the ballet parlour like the cloven hoofs of Fate.

'Where did you come from, Gertrude?'

'Just now I was playing piano for Madame Blavatsky.'

She's a sweet potato but when potatoes go bad, they stink. 'No – forever. You turned up in my life with a broken arm but you existed before that. Everyone's got antecedents – what were yours?'

The dancing feet are as innocent as rain on a roof. 'I was a good girl who married a bad man only to escape and become a piano player. It's not a story you could make a novel from.'

I feint to the right, followed by a quick-switch play, right arm down, left up, then the pirouette, watching her all the time. There's no reaction, nothing but a look of wonder.

'Madame B said you could dance but I had no idea!'

There's no other response, no attack move, no knife. She's nothing but a nice girl with her arms by her sides, amazed at this exhibition of ballet by a 200-pound private detective. I half expect her to ask for an encore. I've still got to put the question.

'Who else is in your life, Match?'

'No-one good. But no-one bad, either. Since escaping from my husband, I've kept away from men. Which means I lead a sequestered life – I get all the kicks I need out of playing piano.'

I'm inclined to believe her; then again I'm inclined to believe anyone beautiful. 'Does the name *Pandora* ring a bell?'

Match half-closes her multi-coloured eyes. 'I know a musical instrument of that name – also called a *tambora*. Or do you mean the chain of jewellery stores?'

'It's neither a musical instrument nor a shop but a person. Someone's been tailing me and I thought it might be you.'

'How long have they been tailing you?'

'About forty years.'

When Gertrude Match puts her hand on my arm it's a pianist's hand and the touch is *legere*. 'I'm thirty-seven, Rainbow. How could I be this Pandora of yours?' After the meaning of life and the best age for whisky it's the only question that really matters. 'Tell me, have you thought of visiting a psychiatrist?'

I leave without saying goodbye.

Chapter 22

THE DAY OF THE DOLLS

Too many hours north of Sydney, the town of Casino's a damp squib and the bus is a slow boat to China. The old man's drunken snores are the grunts of a warthog and Sally can't stop fretting about the chain of events that's landed her where she is. The bus is packed with tourists.

'I feel stupid, exposed and downright *angry*,' she says. 'Remind me again – why are we going wherever we're going?'

'Because I used to live there but also because you're in danger and I made you that way.'

She nods at the old man. 'What about him? Why bring him?'

'Because he could be the answer.'

She turns away. 'If he's the answer, I'd hate to know the question.'

The exhaust system's shot and the bus rattles like a cryptful of bones which means we've got to shout to be heard.

'I'm with her,' the old man mutters. 'I'm here against my will. I'm going back to Melbourne.'

Sally's gone back to looking out the window. What

she sees is verdant countryside but for me there are two landscapes – the one outside the bus and the one in my mind. Trees claw at a manganese sky, the kind that innocence swims in, and pearls fall out of the air. But in my mind it's forty years ago, in a wilderness through which blind memories swirl in a torrent.

I don't know the town because I never went there. I was five when my dad spirited me away from what we kids called the funny farm – the so-called *collective* of hippies situated somewhere outside Nimbin. We lived in a world without fences, real or imagined. We never went to town.

Town is a narrow, pot-holed, tar macadam road lined with a lot of multi-coloured shops, a sign above one of which reads: THE GRASS ON THE OTHER SIDE IS ALWAYS GREENER – WELCOME TO THE OTHER SIDE. As we collect our haversacks, Sally says she's going to stretch her legs and the old man shambles away after her.

'Don't let him near any alcohol,' I tell her. 'He's no good to me drunk.'

She turns and gives me a queer look. 'So now I'm his keeper as well as yours?'

I think I know what she means as I watch them go – the graceful figure of Sally and that of the old man shuffling beside her. Welcome to Paranoia Central.

Someone's playing guitar and I chuck him a couple

of coins at which he jumps to his feet and tries to hug me. 'Wow, thanks, man!' he says with far more enthusiasm than necessary. A sign reads: THIS IS WHERE THE RAINBOW CAFE WAS BEFORE THE FIRE. Stray dogs, more nondescript shops, more hippies pointing guitars at me like machine-guns and a couple of kids in ragged kaftans, their hair in tangles and their thoughts even more tangled.

'Why are we here?' the boy says.

'Because we're dreaming,' the girl replies. 'None of these people are real. We only see what we want to see.'

'What if we don't want to see anything?'

'Then we're not here.'

Nothing makes sense and everything makes complete sense. My fingers close on the dolls in my pocket – the one that Monica said she found at the refuge and the one I found in the house in Melbourne. The kids smell of sweat and the sky's the colour of oxidised slate. The boy nods, I nod back and the girl hugs me. The old man and Sally are dots in the distance.

Notes are sticky-taped to shop windows like magnets on fridges – the Moon's in the ascendant, a guru's doing tea-leaf readings on Tuesday and the reason for all the tourists is the approach of St Valentine's Day. Which to me means a massacre on 14 February 1929 in Chicago presided over by a thug called Al Capone, while to everyone else it means love. The only pub's full and so are the bed and breakfasts. A newspaper flaps against my leg. I pick it up. It contains details of the St Valentine's Day celebrations – market stalls, maypole dances and love-ins. While another story's headed *ANOTHER DEATH* and one of the advertisements for fortune tellers features a picture of a doll much like the ones in my pocket. A joker I ask for directions nods at the paper.

'Valentine's Day is death day,' he says. 'They reckon those deaths are suicides but I know better.'

'I was looking for the fortune teller.'

'You'll find her next door to Luscious Fruit.'

'You're not a believer,' the fortune teller says straight off the bat.

If I hoped she had a wart on her nose and looked cadaverous, I'm disappointed. She's small and full-figured and looks like everyone's grandmother, except for the eyes. We're in a room behind a trinket shop with a sign in the window that says ASTROLOGY, NUMEROLOGY, MEDITATION AND SPIRITUAL HEALING. Dolls are scattered around the room, while a green-baize table stands between me and the necromancer. She's busy trying to set out her cards in the shape of a cross and nearly succeeding.

'What's with the dolls?' I ask her.

'What dolls?'

The dolls that are sprawled on chairs, piled in corners and scattered all over the floor. 'The ones in your advertisement, all these.'

She doesn't look up. 'Oh, I've ceased to be aware of

them except as background to the main event. And they're not really dolls, they're whatever you want them to be.'

'What if I don't want them to be anything?'

In the end it's the eyes – the rest's just bone structure. They're the connie agates of my childhood – the pale-green marbles other kids didn't want because they were too ordinary; eyes that stop her from being a grandmother.

'Choose a card,' she says.

I choose a card. She doesn't even look at it.

'You're a stranger in town and you're searching for your past.' Her fingers touch a card featuring a skeleton; one of its corners is creased. 'This isn't what you think. The Death card doesn't mean death – it stands for regeneration.'

'You've got to say that or risk getting sued.'

'Do you want me to go on or are you just going to sit there making smart comments?'

'Go on,' I reply.

'I see a killer. A killer who's about to get his comeuppance, his just deserts, what's coming to him.' She pauses, frowning. 'That's funny, the cards also say that you don't exist, there's no –'

'Aura.'

'You're making fun of me again, just as you made fun of the dolls. You might come to regret that.' She shakes her head. 'Meanwhile you're not computing. Are you sure ...'

I play along. 'I'm not sure of anything. That's why I'm here.'

Not death but regeneration. Where have I heard that before?

'You had a troubled childhood.' She shivers. 'I hear screams, I see death.' She pales. 'I'm sorry but I can't go on.'

'How about trying?'

The agate eyes close, the mouth opens and I wait for the shaking that will tell me she's in the hands of a Greater Force. Instead she murmurs, 'I see a lot of dancing but it's not happy. People die.'

'I thought you weren't supposed to say stuff like that.'

She opens her eyes without looking at me, gathers the cards and shuffles them. 'I can say whatever I like. Including making the prediction you'll meet a tall, dark stranger and go on a journey.'

She's smiling as she says it but the connie agate eyes don't look up as I leave.

Chapter 23

ALPHA AND OMEGA

I'm outside the pub with two empty whisky glasses before me and nursing a third when a shadow falls across the table with the suns and moons all over it and a hand lights on the back of the chair beside me.

'Anyone using this, my friend?'

A nice, deep voice, the kind that might be owned by a tall, dark stranger but turns out to belong to a small, fat man in crumpled brown corduroy trousers, a green-and-white T-shirt, beige linen jacket and nicely shone shoes with dimples in them. The hair's grey and I put his age at around sixty. There's no hug. Instead he's holding out a hand and smiling.

'The name's Malcolm Booby and I'm a guide.'

A passer-by greets Booby and he flashes his nice, bright smile at them before turning back to me. His hand's so soft it could be a soufflé.

'Hubert Brown,' I murmur.

A drink appears like he conjured it out of thin air. 'You from around here, Herbert?'

It's a test; I correct him. 'It's Hubert. You?'

He no sooner finishes his drink than another

appears. 'I've been here since the Devil was a girl – they call me Mr Nimbin. It's a great place, full of mystery, beauty, soul, energy and health – Paradigm Lost, I call it. You didn't answer my question.'

'No, I didn't.'

The smile jumps out at me like it was lying in ambush. 'I see, you want me to guess. Very well, in your grey tracksuit and windcheater, you've dressed down for the occasion but you're still not from Nimbin. Also I saw you getting off the bus.' He smiles out of his nice grey eyes; the second drink disappears; someone else greets him; he nods in reply then returns his gaze to me like it never went away as a third drink arrives – plus a whisky for me.

'It's a nice day.'

I'm not here to talk about the weather. 'Know where we can find a bed, Booby?'

'How many of you are there?'

I'm about to say, *I'm a detective, a father, a son, a paranoid schizophrenic, an ex-husband, a non-person and a misanthrope – which would make it about seven,* but think better of it. And while I'm thinking better of it, Sally and the old man roll in like a Bondi thumper. Booby's on his feet in an instant.

'You must be Mrs Brown.' He glances at the old man. 'While you'll be –'

The old man slumps in the chair that Booby just vacated. 'I'll be stuffed,' he says. 'Where's me beer.'

'You're not getting one,' I tell him. 'You're drying out.'

'All right, a fag then.'

'No.'

'Who do you think you are?'

'He's been pestering me for a drink ever since we arrived,' Sally says. 'Much more interesting drugs were on offer but he didn't have any money.'

The old man turns on her. 'And you wouldn't give me any.'

Booby intervenes. 'How long are you in town?'

The old man glares at Booby. 'And who the hell –'

He suddenly seems to think better of it, shrugs like it's not worth the candle and Booby calmly continues like the old man hasn't spoken, like he isn't even there.

'I only ask because if you haven't anywhere else to go you can stay with us. And if you're here for the weekend, you might like to attend our little St Valentine's Day celebration.' He waves aside any protests before we can make them. 'We haven't got the phone on so I can't ring my wife to warn her but as long as we don't arrive too early I'm sure it'll be fine.' He speaks like he's done this before but also like he's trying to reassure himself. 'That gives us a couple of hours. How about a spin in the Maserati?'

The Maserati is an old Ford Transit van with *BOOBY'S TOURS* in black on the side but it gets the old man away from the pub. Booby waves through a dusty window at a park with a rainbow-coloured building in the middle of it. 'That's the community centre and next door's the radio station.'

'Fascinating,' Sally says like it's not fascinating at all.

The candle factory's well worth a visit, there's a place called the Nowhere Café, a lot of interesting shops and even more interesting people, all set in Nature's wonderland. Which brings us to Nature's wonderland. The old man stays slouched like a small boy with the sulks while me, Sally and Booby teeter on the edge of a cliff.

'Not long ago that valley used to be an ocean,' Booby says, his voice heavy with conviction. 'Over there's Mount Wollumbin – it used to be a volcano.' Molten lava's pouring down the sides and survivors are fleeing, their hair on fire, screaming. *I hear screams,* the necromancer said. *I see death.*

By tour's end it's late afternoon and me, Sally and Booby are in the front of the van while the old man's alone with his devils in the back. He's not happy but he never is. Booby's pitching a yarn that's a mix of fact and fiction, pre-history and magic, with a bit of religion thrown in for good measure – an unholy trinity of Darwin, *The Golden Bough* and the Bible. He reminds me of the necromancer. He also reminds me of my mother.

At one point his mobile rings and he stops the van, climbs out and answers it. I hear his deep, sonorous voice murmur something but can't make out what it is. The tour and the commentary have brought it all back – my mother rattling on about spirituality, preaching about Earth Spirits and spouting random scraps of poetry ending in a row of dots like it meant something when it didn't.

'You've made quite a study of this,' Sally says as Booby finishes his call and climbs back into the van.

Booby inclines his head. 'When humans evolved

from fishes, we climbed out of the sea. We mock the Aboriginal Dreamtime but that's only because the unknown scares us. We feel safer looking down on others' beliefs, just as we looked down into that valley back there. We need to confront our fears and burnish our spirit in the flames so we can renew ourselves.'

Sally changes the subject. 'Have you always lived here?'

'I wouldn't live anywhere else.'

'Why?'

'Because this is the beginning and the end, alpha and omega, fundamental to both our existence and our non-existence. Only in somewhere like Nimbin can we hope to get in touch with our real selves.' He smiles gently. 'But I mustn't get too serious – I get the feeling your husband doesn't approve.'

It's the second time he's married us but Sally doesn't correct him.

A car's following us. A pair of thugs attacked me at the refuge followed by a second attack at Rory's, someone tried to kill Sally, and Hell and Damnation's dead. I don't know if I'm a killer or why all of a sudden the old man's fallen silent or how long before the stuff I want out of his addled brain is going to come to the surface. All I know is that I need some information and need it bad.

We didn't get about in cars in my childhood – the ride to Sydney was my first in anything other than a billy cart and the trip in Booby's van reminds me of it. *We can put you up,* Booby said. It's an offer too good to be true. But darkness is falling and it hasn't proved true yet.

'I'm sorry, I must be boring you silly,' Booby says, breaking the silence. 'What about you? What line of business are you in, Herbert?'

This time I don't bother correcting him. 'Market research. I find out how people vote, what they're interested in and what they buy.'

It's a conversation stopper; it's meant to be. 'Fascinating.' Booby turns to Sally. 'And you?'

'I paint.'

'And you, old fellow, who's so quiet in the back?'

But there's no reply from the old fellow in the back.

Chapter 24

BECAUSE OF THE BATS

Up to now the countryside's been lush greenery, the kind you could drown in – the chrome and viridian of mature gums and the peppermint of saplings darkening to the somnolent depths of Prussian-green mangroves. Lantana and morning glory weave among native plants like boa constrictors and now and again there's the paler green of camphor laurels.

But as darkness falls, the shades fade to earth colours – burnt madder, indian red, raw umber and violet. The ultramarine sky is shot through with flames like the volcano's suddenly become active, molten lava spewing down its sides as the sun deals the landscape its parting blow, while survivors flee from the volcano with their hair on fire.

I open the window to dispel my thoughts and that's when I hear the squeaks. It's the sound of rusty wheels, of seized bearings, a multitude of rats. No, not rats – bats. Because there are suddenly thousands of them unleashed by the coming night, black ash against a pewter sky, a vortex soaring up from the Moreton Bay figs, the rustle of their wings the crackling flames of an inferno. Booby points out a stone formation rising above the trees.

'That's Nimbin Rocks.'

I'm back in my childhood, in the hut thrown together by my father – my father who's now the old man hunched and silent in the back. I'm curled on my straw bed petrified, ready with the scissors to cut off the bats' legs, shaking with fear because – apart from my sister – I'm alone. It's Mum's special night, she said before she left, and any significance I apply to that now has got to be nothing but déjà vu. I was a kid, there were bats and I had to protect my sister.

A wooden gate hangs off its hinges and blackberries and lantana claw at the van's sides. I pull in my arm. The headlight – only one's working – cuts a swath through the darkness. Black shapes appear out of nowhere.

This is where Pandora dates from. The van's single headlamp illuminates a track as narrow as a monomaniac's thoughts. That night, I remember being grabbed by my father, stuffed in a van and taken on a journey something like this. Until we ended up at Aunt Rube's – me, the old man who's now behind me and his blonde. A truck hurtles past, interrupting my thoughts.

'How long have you lived in Nimbin?' Sally asks, picking up a conversation from a couple of kilometres back.

'Several years or several centuries, who knows? We call it Nimbin time.'

The track leads under the feature called Nimbin Rocks, the van's single headlight probing like the eye of a Cyclops. A fox slinks across the road, its red eyes glistening; a kangaroo bounces alongside; and something black – an owl, a bat or a pterodactyl – covers the windscreen before banking away. We've been on this road forever. Nimbin time.

Booby resumes his travelogue. 'As you may or may not know, a number of the old collectives are still in existence. They were all the go in the 1970s. We didn't aim to be great farmers – we wanted to create a new world. That's Nature Farm over there and the one to your left is the Carbourne Collective.'

Black hills sweep away on either side. Nothing seemed *aimed at* when we were kids. When I grazed my knee, got a bunged-up nose or cut my hand, the stranger who happened across me would say something like: *It was meant to be.* And maybe take me home or maybe not. There were mantras and mandalas and talk of Nimbin time as though we inhabited another planet, a place where time didn't exist – just space and plenty of it.

'We're almost there.'

We arrive at an overgrown driveway, a rickety bridge, more bumps even than on the road; the tentacles of out-of-control blackberries, lantana and morning glory reach out for as we plunge deeper into the darkness. Sally's politeness underlines her hostility – towards me, towards Booby, towards the old man.

'It looks like a war zone,' she murmurs. 'What happened?'

Decrepit buildings appear in the beam of the headlight only to disappear again – crazy structures covered with weeds and once-bright graffiti; the tattered remains of tents and teetering things of wood; ancient caravans; concrete bunkers; a windmill with half its vanes missing; a house with *oeil de boeuf* windows, the glass shattered; rusty containers with the shapes of what might once have been solar panels dangling from their roofs. Booby's mobile phone rings but he doesn't answer it. Instead he stops the van, his fingers tightening on the wheel. His hands seem much older than the rest of him.

'I've been thinking.' He's staring straight ahead. 'What if I let you out here? It used to be some kind of hostel – what we used to call the Palais Royale.'

A long, low, ramshackle building stretches before us.

'Fantastic,' Sally says.

Booby shakes his head; he's changed his mind. 'No, a promise is a promise.'

He restarts the van, crunches it into gear and we drive on. As if on impulse, he takes a paper bag off the dashboard and hands around what he calls 'Nimbin lollies'. Even the old man takes one but he'd take anything. The sweets taste of aniseed. More dwellings – a few with lights on but most not; more blackberries; and finally a sedate structure with an old car parked out the front and, off to the right, a huge pile of garbage teetering under the weight of old tyres. I make out what looks like an agricultural experiment gone wrong – bars and boxes, rough-hewn poles, raised garden beds, scarecrows. The road ahead veers off to the left. The brakes screech as Booby pulls up.

'Now for the naked wife,' he says.

We climb down, stiff after the long ride. I go to retrieve the backpacks but Booby stops me.

'It wouldn't be a good look, turning up as if you

expect to stay. We'll do it in stages.'

The house looks like it was designed before the invention of right angles – something between a backyard dunny and a cathedral. A bark roof sags over corrugated-iron walls supported by buttresses and surrounded by a makeshift verandah. Gothic windows throw multi-coloured light onto pavers while late violets bloom by the slab-wood door.

The old man hovers while Booby enters the house. 'Let's see how she blows,' he says.

She's not what I expect but we'd be something of a surprise to her, too, a large woman in her sixties, her grey hair blonded, wearing a bulky kaftan.

'At least she's clothed,' Sally murmurs, then aloud to Booby: 'Aren't you going to introduce us?'

'This is Mr and Mrs Brown and' – he looks around – 'somewhere outside is an old man.'

Sally steps forward, smiling. 'Whatever Malcolm says, we're not married – in fact we hardly know each other. I'm Sheila, this is Hubert and the old gentleman outside calls himself Sam. We're visiting Nimbin because we have some time to kill. It's very kind of you to put us up.'

The old man hasn't come in. If you run away when your wife kills herself, you're not going to return forty years later, laughing. Booby's wife has the look of an ageing hippy still trying to cling to her youth, her face is expressionless and her eyes are hard. She turns to her husband. 'Could I see you for a moment, Malcolm?'

They pass through an internal doorway, leaving me and Sally alone with adze-cut rafters, a wood-burning stove that doubles as a heater, a telephone which must be some kind of prop, too many bad paintings, a rammed-earth floor and the feeling we're not wanted. The place is in disarray – a chair's lying on its side, the table's skewiff and the floor's wet like it's just been mopped. The happy couple returns. Booby shuffles his feet while his wife glares at me.

'You've caused us a lot of trouble,' she says.

'Calm down, Marsha,' Booby says; it sounds like a warning.

She turns on him. 'Why should I calm down – or, rather, why should I *pretend*? We ought to be allowed to express our true feelings, there's far too much namby-pamby evasion in this world.'

Booby turns to us, his expression one of apologetic resignation. 'I'll drop you at the gate.'

As we leave, the phone starts ringing but stops when Marsha answers it.

Chapter 25

BODY OF EVIDENCE

I climb out of the van into darkness and open the side door while Sally retrieves the packs. Booby stays where he is – his hands on the steering wheel, staring straight ahead even though there's nothing to stare at. For some reason, the headline from the newspaper jumps into my head like a newly-opened pop-up shop: *ANOTHER DEATH*.

I'm here to find Pandora. Any other bodies are someone else's problem, someone else's unexplained corpses. My mother and my sister died on a burning windmill and the totem poles are where it occurred. I step back as Booby leaves in a cloud of dust. One of his taillights doesn't work either.

I'm in a weed-infested outpost of civilisation looking for a phantom with an old man who's probably my father and a woman who hates me. *Don't leave the windows open or you'll get bats in your hair.* My mother was mad and my father gutless. *Your mother probably took drugs during pregnancy,* the shrink said. *Your enemies are all in your head.* I should have left them there.

Sally's just about dead on her feet and the old man

looks even more of a zombie than usual. It's too late to go back to town and there's nowhere to stay there anyway. I make for the nearest building, the one Booby called the Palais Royale. I'm not so far gone that I'm going in without checking. The sense of Pandora is strong – this is where it all began, in this hive of shadows. Booby drove off without a word, his single taillight bouncing like a scarlet firefly. 'Wait here,' I say.

The moonlight illuminates an architectural horror story, a building that's run as wild as the lantana. It's a long, low, negative shape outlined against a sky of ultramarine violet. A hundred paces from end to end, its crenate roofline is broken by onion domes, a pitched slate roof, iron skillions, the odd spire. There are no doors to the side, just glassless windows. A sign on a stump has been altered to read: *PALLIASSE ROYAL*. It's a haunted house, the motel from *Psycho*, the stuff of nightmares.

But that's a string of clichés and clichés never solved anything. I get a torch out of my pack and go in, the walls closing around me like tentacles. The rooms are linked by a series of drunken passageways, the place part crumbling concrete, part rotten wood, with some walls of hardened mud while others are wooden slabs, rough-cut when the timber was still green and now separating. I run into a spider's web and something's got under my shirt. A snake blinks in the smoky beam of the torch. On the walls swastikas mingle with peace insignia and stars of David. The torchlight flickers.

My mother might have been mad but she wasn't alone in her fantasies. Roughcast depictions of rainbows are everywhere – together with what might be spatters of blood, a tree, an arrow, a cross. Drawings that once might have meant something are incoherent daubings by Dali wannabes. The floor's broken concrete with weeds sprouting from the cracks. I make my way past broken cupboards, scattered pots, piles of clothing – emerging at the southern end where I call out to Sally. There's no response.

I hardly know her, only that she's that most dangerous of combinations – beautiful and angry. I don't even know the old man. I'm stumbling around in the dark with a pair of strangers and my voice is swallowed by darkness. What did I hope to prove by coming to Nimbin? That I'm not mad? I've proved I'm mad just by coming here.

'Where are you?' I call. 'Sally? Sheila? Old man? Sam? Answer me, will you!'

But they've gone and suddenly I'm a child again. Bats wheel around my head, panic seizes me and dark things rear out of the darkness – half-memories, imaginings, fears. The windmill's turning again and my mother's screaming – my mother and my sister. My head spins. Pandora.

I don't know what happened. Only that I wake blinking in blackness. I must have tripped or the emotion got too much for me or I've had some kind of fantasy reaction to being in Nimbin. I can't feel any bumps on my head and I'm not bleeding. All I know is that I'm staggering to my feet and there's a strong sense that time has passed. I can't find the torch and my head's splitting.

Aunt Rube: *Anchor yourself. Think of what you know. Find a line of thought and follow it, untangle the knots, relax.* But I can't do any of that. Because in my mind, Sally is tangled up with my mother, my sister, Tsunami, Gertrude Match, Ariadne, Hélène Dalmatian, Monica Best, Denise, Annie and Salina. And each and every one of them could be Pandora. *You could kill someone close to you.* I switch thought lines.

What do I know about Sally? What do I know about any of them? I confronted all of them and they all claimed to be innocent. And how could any of them except Ariadne be Pandora? They're all too young. Like the shrink said, it's all in my mind. I'm mad. Pandora never existed. I reel away from the possibilities. In Nimbin, memories are the smell of lantana.

I blunder into a bush and my foot nudges against something soft. The odour's that of an animal. There's a body and in context it must be some creature that's met with a bad end. We saw them by the roadside on the way here, victims of vehicles and/or bullets. Humans like killing and wombats don't shoot back. But this body's bigger than that of a wombat – much bigger.

Baseless assumptions are bumps in the road of detecting and you try to avoid them. Or if you can't avoid them, accept them for what they're worth and work your way around them without banging your head against a brick wall. I bend and my fingers touch cloth. It's not a wombat. *ANOTHER DEATH,* the newspaper said.

My first assumption is that it's Mr Whimsy Baldface – Malcolm Booby. Second: that it's that creeping derelict, my putative father. And – *desperately not,* I find myself begging – the body of Sally. But if it's any of them, why is he or she lying here dead? And who killed him or her?

That's when I entertain the fourth assumption – no, not assumption, *the very real possibility* – and start shaking. *Whoever belongs to the body, I made it that way.* I know from experience that lack of consciousness is the killer's favourite defence. *I blacked out and when I came to there was blood on my hands and this body lying on the ground. I don't remember a thing.*

Before technology appropriated the name, black-berries were bushes. I drag them aside. The moon and stars are undimmed by city lights and after I lost the torch my rods and cones started adjusting to the dark. But everything's still obscure – what happened, what's in front of me. The body's on the ground with red blackberries covering its face – alizarin crimson against black leaves. All I can make out are two wide-awake eyes and the red berries.

I touch one of the eyes and it doesn't blink. *ANOTHER DEATH.* I run my hands down the body to the feet. It's a big corpse, hard-muscled and dressed in denim jacket and jeans, its sideways hip upthrust. People are the clothes they wear, never more so than when they're dead. And this person's very dead. I place a hand on the ground to steady myself and peer into the darkness, hoping to see the killer. My fingers close on something.

There was no shout, no scream, no indication of who it was but I know this body must be Sally's and that I killed her. I try to do the visual but can't. I'm blind again but this time it's tears. *You might end up killing someone you love.* I blacked out – why, I don't know. What happened after I blacked out I don't know, either. And even if I didn't kill her, I'm still the cause of her death. I allowed myself to be followed to Hobart where she was shot at by the people who followed me, then I brought her here and now she's dead. I expected to find Pandora so why couldn't Pandora have found me first? Either that or *I'm* Pandora. My vision's warped like that of a criminal adjusting to life outside after a long sentence. It was Pandora. If it wasn't, I'm mad and it was me.

I know now why I brought Sally here. It wasn't just to keep her safe although that was one of the reasons. It was because I wanted her nearby so she could keep an eye on me. Caligari was right – I'm a killer. *Sally!* I called. But I was calling the dead. And somewhere not far away my newfound *paterfamilias* is probably also lying dead because I killed him, too. Only he'll be less mourned – by the world, by me. *TWO MORE DEATHS,* the heading will read. Deaths that occurred after I blacked out.

I take a breath. *Watch out for the bats,* my mother

warned me. But it's not the bats, it's me. With a body that I can't – don't want to – identify. *Keep the cases separate,* Monica Best warned. But it's like my mother's warning about the bats. *The scissors are by your bed,* she said. The bats are my fears and my weapons are my hands. A past littered with deaths when I thought I'd killed nobody; Sally accusing me of killing one of her patients; Hélène Dalmatian with a bullet in her brain and me holding the smoking gun …

I slip the thing I picked up into my pocket. You can ignore memories but you can't hide the facts. Not when they're right in front of you, not when your latest victim's staring you in the face.

Chapter 26

BLOOD ON THE BLACKBERRIES

'What on earth are you doing?'

It's Sally's voice yet the corpse is still there, its eyes wide open and staring. Bats rise against the night sky. Someone's waving a torch.

'Where's the old man?' I barely recognise my own voice. 'Pass me your torch.'

The mist coils in the beam as she hands it to me. I haven't done *cause of death* because I'm afraid of what I might find. *Look before you leap and always remember you've got the option of not leaping at all.* I probe with the torchlight as well as with my hand but keep my eyes off the face because I'm afraid of what I'll see. I force myself to look down.

It was a knife to the throat – left side – leaving blood on the blackberries. Because the blackberries aren't red at all and if I hadn't been so close I would have realised. It's the second week in February, a few days before St Valentine's Day – February 14 – late summer, and this far north the berries would no longer be red but their eponymous colour – black. Blood on the blackberries, ashes to ashes, and the blood's still red. I glance up at Sally. In the darkness she looks a lot bigger than she is and far more dangerous than I care to remember.

'Where were you?'

'I think I had some kind of dizzy spell,' she says. 'Not surprising after all that's happened.'

'What about the old man?'

'I think he wandered off.'

'Wandered off *where*?'

The old man emerges like a wraith. 'I'm here, son.'

It's not who I expect but it's never who you expect because you don't want to expect anyone. I go into investigator mode because that way I can forget – for the moment anyway – who and what I'm investigating. It's a run-of-the-mill autopsy, I tell myself, and the body on the bench with the blood-drain around it is no-one I know. There's the wound to the side of the neck and swinging the torch away from those staring eyes, there are the marks. The shirt's top three buttons are undone and the shirt's pulled open. I've got to notice that because it's my job to notice. But at the same time I sense that even in death – no, *especially* in death – there should be privacy. Because a corpse is like a child, innocent and vulnerable, and bodies should keep their secrets. I feel like a violator.

At first I mistake the marks for primitive drawings, those stick figures kids make using stones in the ground, with circles for heads and lines for torsos and limbs, because kids reduce what they see to basics. But these marks weren't made in hard ground but in soft flesh and they're not figures but words. Number of letters: eleven. Dimensions: roughly an inch high – 2.5 centimetres in the new money – and scratched to the depth of the width of a small coin. Blood that's only just now blackening. Implement employed –

'Would you mind coming here for a moment, Sally?'

'What is it?'

I indicate the marks with the torch. 'What do the words say?'

She gives them a cursory glance. '*Tyrannosaur* or something. But is this really the time to be playing detective? Shouldn't we report it?' She straightens. 'Whatever crazy adventure you're on can't have anything to do with this. The death clearly wasn't due to natural causes. We should notify the police.'

I hold out the torch and she takes it, gripping it as she might a scalpel as she squats. She criss-crosses the corpse's chest with the beam, finally bringing it back to the marks.

'No, it's not *TYRANNOSAUR*. It's more like *TRAN NESOL* – whatever that means – followed by the numeral *10*. The implement used wasn't sharp, which rules out anything like a scalpel.'

'How can you tell?'

'The edges of the incisions are rough. See there, there and there? They're rips rather than cuts. It was something like an old-fashioned tin-opener or a blunt knife. It might even have been a fork. There was no bleeding, which means the wounds were inflicted *after* death.'

'Why were the marks made?'

'In my work I've seen the work of madmen. But this isn't the work of a madman. It's as if the killer's trying to tell us something.'

Chapter 27

CUT AND RUN

She sits back. 'It reminds me of the so-called magic tricks that *shalyuns* – Brazilian witchdoctors – perform in order to instil fear in people. I think the words are intended to invoke the kind of questions we're asking. Prehistoric man made marks in caves. Was it art or did they want to convey information?' Sally shivers and draws back even further. 'But these marks are brutal.' She glances at me. 'They remind me of the bullet you put in that man's skull, the one I operated on.'

'What do you mean – brutal?'

'It's as if the killer was fighting forces beyond reason.'

'And the cause of death?'

She brings the torchlight up to the corpse's neck. 'The carotid artery was severed. Death would have been instantaneous.'

I've checked the arms for defensive wounds – there are none; and under the fingernails for cloth, blood, skin – ditto. And while checking the arms I also came across the same *non-watch* that Hélène Dalmatian was wearing when she died.

'Was the same implement used on the chest as on the neck?'

She shakes her head. 'The words were an add-on extra and the weapon used was blunt while the incision to the neck was clean.'

'In your opinion were the words on the chest carved *just after* death or much later?'

'I can't tell.'

'How long has she been dead?'

'Not my field – I'm a surgeon not a zetetic. Death could have occurred anywhere from a few minutes to a few hours ago. It's a cold night.'

I know the answer but I still ask. 'Was she killed here?'

'Hard to say.' She frowns. 'But what's it got to do with me? This is *your* field. You knew her, didn't you?'

'Yeah, I knew her.'

'Is she an old friend from Nimbin or someone who followed us? Was she on the bus or was she lying in wait?' It's a surgeon's probing, a surgeon who needs an accurate diagnosis before proceeding further, before applying the scalpel.

'She was an insurance agent I met a long time ago and whose acquaintance I remade only recently. She was sacked because of something I did – or didn't do. Her name is Monica Best.'

At times like these you've got two choices. You can cut and run or you can stay and listen to the music

– in this case, Schubert's *Death and the Maiden.*
Which means I've got no choice at all because music
there will be. This might be Nimbin but there are
still laws and there are still cops and they'll come
running like blood from a severed artery when they
learn about the corpse because that's how they're
built.

A tourist on an early-morning jog will stumble
upon the body and call the cops on his ever-handy
mobile. And the first thing the cops will *want* to say
is, *Don't touch anything.* Except they won't say that
because there's something even more important
than not touching anything and that's the identity
of the caller. *Who are you?* they'll ask, adding: *We
only need your name for the records.* Except that's not
why they need the name at all. They need the name
because the caller's the first cab off the rank, the
suspect-in-chief, the person of most interest in their
investigation. Until someone of even more interest
comes along.

After that they'll follow procedure, which is:
1. Inspect the corpse;
2. Interrogate the natives. During which they'll
    get around to interviewing Booby and –
    willingly or unwillingly – he'll say he dropped
    us where the body was found – a criminal, a
    derelict and an elegant dame out of place in
    that company. The cops will work back from
    there. Say what you like about cops, they
    follow procedure. Under questioning, Booby
    will tell them the suspects just arrived in
    Nimbin; then
3. Talk to the driver of the bus and the

passengers.

And in so doing find that the trio boarded the bus in Casino after travelling by train from Sydney. The tickets will be by far the best lead to our identity. Country Rail, State Rail, Rack and Pinion or simply Rack Off – whatever they call themselves now – will say who bought them and under what names. Trips have to be booked and the names logged into a computer. We gave false names but that's the best lead of all. *We want to fingerprint your van,* the cops will tell Booby. They'll find our prints, no trouble at all. After so many years on the streets the old man's will be in files everywhere while Sally's will match those of a person who disappeared from a witness protection program. And mine will be all over everything – a suddenly not-so-anonymous detective.

All of which means I can't call the cops. Because if I do they'll do two things pretty well simultaneous – they'll trace the call and at the same time hurry to the scene of the crime before anyone has a chance to interfere with the evidence. But more important still, to stop the caller doing a runner. They'll think I killed her and all they'll need after that is a motive. That will be harder but they'll still find one. The corpse's fingerprints will match those of a security officer at a refuge, prints the cops will already have because all security personnel are fingerprinted. A cross-check will produce a court case involving the same security officer during which the following questions were asked. *You say there was a private detective involved in this case. What was his name? Can you describe him?* And the description will bear an uncanny resemblance to the person who – in company with two others – was dropped near the body of the woman who lost the court case because of the detective ...

Making ourselves scarce is a lottery ticket but we've got to buy it.

'Where are we going?' Sally asks. 'We have to call the police.'

I retrieve the torch. 'Only if you want the people hunting for you to find you. Rank amateurs can monitor police radios and the Mafia are far from amateurs. Besides which, we're at a murder scene which means we've got to get out of here – fast.'

Monica Best was a chief starter to be Pandora. Why was she in Nimbin and why is she dead? More importantly, who killed her?

Chapter 28

ISLAND OF MADNESS

There's no great flash of inspiration – nothing but a sense of strangeness, a memory of hippies finding a kid with a grazed knee and murmuring trite uncertainties like: *It was meant to be.* That and the bats. I was five, for Christ's sake, no more than a kid. And in those days – those glorious, inglorious seventies – kids were Nazis: born to be borne, something to be seen and not heard, an evil to be put up with or put down.

The Mafia's after Sally; the people who killed Hélène Dalmatian and were waiting at Rory's are after me; Pandora's here somewhere; and now there'll be cops. I don't need to be paranoid to know I'm being followed. But I can't be distracted from the main game – and that is proving Pandora exists. I need to think myself into the case. *Method detecting,* Rube called it.

We're heading for the hills – for no reason other than the hills are elsewhere. Before us, Nimbin Rocks – grim, dark and foreboding – are black holes in a violet sky. I've kept the old man away from the grog and he's suffering because of it. With his hair cut and in clean clothes he looks halfway respectable. But he's still the same bastard who ran off when his wife and daughter were dying – a drunk, a blackmailer, a coward. I don't want him anywhere near me but there's no such thing as *want*. He knows where we lived, where it happened, *what* happened and the identity of my nemesis. He's a metal detector, a geiger counter, a sniffer dog – the key to finding Pandora. Which is why Sally's here. I might be keeping her out of the hands of the Mafia but she's also keeping an eye on me. And since the discovery of the body, something's changed. It's like she's worked something out. I expected her to become even more distant. Instead, on the occasions when we accidentally brush against one another, she no longer draws away.

Then again, it's probably just my imagination.

The going's steep and every few minutes the old man demands a drink. Sally produces a Rum Crunch chocolate bar while my mind toggles between the problems of not getting tangled in the lantana and who killed Monica Best. Correction: Monica Best and Hélène Dalmatian. The dolls in my pocket – the doll that Monica found outside the refuge and the one from my father's place of refuge in Melbourne – have been joined by the one I just found next to the latest body.

Shadow is substance and substance shadow while behind every tree I imagine the cops, the mystery killer, the Mafia and/or Pandora. *How can any of those women be Pandora if she existed forty years ago?* But when shadow is substance anything's possible. *You see what you want to see,* the necromancer said. I hurry the old man along with more roughness than necessary. Rabbits and wombats have dug holes in our path like the hole I've dug for myself. The old man's angry because I've dragged him through a patch of nettles.

'I need a drink,' he grumbles.

I turn away. *Why are we doing this?* I asked Rube whenever she took me off into the bush. *Because one day you might need to survive in the wild,* she replied. *You've read the book, now put what you've learnt into practice. Survive.*

It's summer but the night was cold and the old man missed his liquor. In the bright light of morning I find Sally's fashioned a broom out of twigs and is sweeping stones, bones and bat droppings out of the cave while I scavenge for food. A kookaburra laughs and somewhere a magpie warbles. The remains of our breakfast lie among the stones. The old man has refused food – *I'm not eating any of that crap,* he muttered. All he wants is something to drink. I look down into the valley at the scattered farmlets. From the perspective of the cave there are no trees, just green cottonwool and from the perspective of years, memories as soft as the bush. In my mind my childhood was danger free.

'You keep saying we're escaping from the Mafia but where are they?' Sally asks. 'And that's not all, is it? That body has a lot to do with why we're here.' Her eyes fix on mine. 'All those years ago you solved my case but now you can't even solve your own.' It's not an accusation – it's a fact. 'Who was she?'

'She was a case that went wrong. I solved the case but left her to pick up the pieces. The matter went to court and she was caught in the cross-fire. She lost her job because I wasn't there to help.'

'But *who* was she?'

'How would I know? A private eye never knows anyone. She's just another dame with a past.'

'One thing's for certain, she doesn't have a future.' Sally pushes her fists deep in her pockets. 'Was there anything between you? Did you love her? People kill for love.'

From the mouth of the cave the world goes on forever – the pale sky contains even paler clouds and below us are the deep blues, greens and yellows of an ocean of time. Without booze the old man looks like death warmed up, his face wearing an expression of malevolence as he emerges back into a world he's been trying to escape. For the first time I almost recognise him. Nothing physical – it's his air of contempt, like he's no longer a piece of flotsam scraped off a Melbourne street but a man who's worked out the meaning of life and everyone else is stupid.

'Look at us,' he sneers. 'A bunch of bloody reffos in a cave in the middle of la-la land.' He waves his skinny arms – the cave ceiling's just high enough not to bruise his knuckles. 'Who's *she*? And you're not my son – what makes you think you are?'

Suddenly I know. It's not the face or even the voice that tells me it's him. It's the *attitude* of a man who thinks he's right even when he knows otherwise. Who screamed and shouted and made my mother's life hell. Who cleared out, leaving others to clean up the mess. If the cops ever interviewed him about what happened that night, it would have been cursory. Because it was Nimbin they'd already decided it was suicide, possibly drug-induced. I ignore the old man's ravings.

'You brought me with you because you compromised my safety,' Sally says. 'I understand that. But why him?'

'My childhood's here somewhere and as soon as the old man's dried out he'll lead me to it. And when I get to that place of tepees, windmills and Easter Island statues, I'll have the answer.'

'The answer to what?'

'Pandora's identity and where I can find her.'

'But why do you need to find this Pandora?'

'To prove I'm not mad.'

'And after you find her what then? Do you go back to being what you were? Do I go back into the witness protection program? And if I do, will I be safe? Will I ever practise surgery again? Do you destroy everyone you meet?'

'Humans can go weeks without food but not without water. I'll go find some.'

But before I leave, I find the whitener I asked her
to buy and pomade my hair.

Chapter 29

INTO THE VALLEY OF DEATH

I told Sally I was going to look for water. It wasn't a lie but before that I've got to go into town and before that again I've got to check the body. Criminals return to the scene of the crime except I can't accept it was *my* crime. I left Sally with instructions to:

1. Keep an eye on the old man like a murderer watches an intended victim because he'll try to escape; and
2. Gather berries, fungi, roots, et cetera, that might be edible.

There's no movement apart from occasional grunts followed by the *thump-thump-thump* of marsupials, the rustle of lizards and the flapping of wings. If the cops don't know yet, I've got time – not much but some. I touch the dolls in my pocket. The old man might be the key. But first I've got to find the lock.

It looked easy. The cave gave onto an accommodating landscape in which I could make out the Palais Royale. All I had to do was head for the spire. I check the position of the sun and alter course. No fires, I told Sally, either inside the cave or out. The food can be eaten raw but not before I get back.

The corpse has gone.

I don't need to check my bearings. The building's to my right and this is the blackberry bush but there's no corpse. It introduces a new factor into the equation only I'm not sure what it is. The police didn't take the body because they haven't been here. There's no plastic tape indicating a crime scene; no patchwork of overlapping tyre tracks; no boot prints; no body tracing; no-one on guard duty.

In the Palais Royale I come across a billy and a saucepan.

There's a lot of traffic because of the coming St Valentine's Day festival and I get a ride within minutes. I don't buy food because it would only tell Sally where I've been. The paper shop's halfway along Main Street.

'You're lucky there are any left,' the bloke behind the counter says. 'These tourists are like bloody locusts.'

'How much?'

'They come to gawp at the hippies but all they get is the censored version – the didgeridoos, the hugs, the drugs, the markets and the maypoles.'

'Would two bucks cover it?'

'There's talk of secret rites and sacrifices.'

Tourists jostle me as I leaf through the newspaper. There was no corpse, Monica Best didn't die and the cops aren't after us. Someone nudges against me but it's just another hugger.

'Did you find it, man?'

'Find what?' I say.

'Futility, man. That's what everyone's after, isn't it?' The hippy giggles. 'Or in your case, the card reader. You were looking for her, weren't you?' He frowns. 'Anyway, she was looking for you.'

It's the joker who gave me directions. Someone must pay him to keep an eye on tourists. What he's told me might be nothing but nothing's a lot more than I've got. And nothing says I can't pay a return visit to her while I'm here. The sign's still in the window and she's still in the room beyond the sign. But when I look around the dolls have gone.

'Where are they?'

The dame's got her back to me and she doesn't look around. 'Where are what?'

'The dolls.'

'What dolls?'

I change tack. 'Why did you want to see me?'

She's silent for a moment. Then, 'Non-believers think we seers are all flush and bluster. What they *don't* know is that we can be proactive. When someone makes an appointment we find out about them before they arrive – in that regard, the internet has made our lives a whole lot easier. But in your case I found nothing and so naturally I ask myself why.'

'It's because there's nothing to discover.'

When I emerge into the street, Booby's hail-fellow-well-meeting someone across the road. This is Nimbin and in Nimbin people are friendly. I don't read the writing on the side of the four-wheel-drive vehicle as I climb in. Three men are inside, all of them wearing white, all of them big, all of them not to get in a vehicle with. I recognise the one in the back but he doesn't remember me. Disguise is a lot more than a change of hair colour. I've rounded my shoulders and developed a squint.

'You a local?' he asks.

'Yeah.'

'Then you might be able to help us. We're looking for someone who'd be trying to pass himself off as a tourist but who's really an escapee from a lunatic asylum. He's big like you but a lot younger and with certain characteristics you don't possess. He'd be wearing bright clothes and a hat.' He fishes in a pocket and pulls out a card. 'Call this number if you happen to see him.'

Disguise is the way you talk and my voice is a croak. 'I take it you're the law.'

'Something like that,' the man in the white coat replies.

I croak to them to let me out and stagger away. Old people don't run and neither do the innocent. The writing on the card matches the writing on the side of the four-wheel drive: *SIDONIA CLINIC.*

It's past midday by the time I return. Whoever killed Monica Best is still around – plus the Mafia and Pandora and now also the goons from the clinic. I've picked up the pot and pan from the Palais Royale, filled the pot at a creek and done my best to hide my tracks – crossing and recrossing the creek, doubling back, walking sideways, hopping, skipping and jumping. It creates an appetite but Sally's resourceful – she will have found something.

The old man's crouching in the rear of the cave and in the mouth of the cave Sally's carving up what she's foraged. 'Where have you been?' she asks.

'Water's like a good woman,' I reply, 'hard to find.' It gets me the first smile I've seen from her in a long time. 'What did you get?'

I chuck the fungi to one side. 'Fungus kills you or at least puts you in Fantasyland – a lot of mushrooms are hallucinogenic. There are good ones and there are bad ones. For example this is the deadly *Amanita*. See those white gills? Very few *safe* mushrooms possess white gills. Also there's a collar around the stalk – no edible mushroom has a collar around its stalk. Then there's the *volva* or skirt …'

She breaks in, 'Along with a great many other subjects, I studied alternative medicine. As a doctor I'm aware humans need starch, protein and fat. The blackberry, *Rubus Fruticosus*, is wonderful because we can eat all parts of it. This is Bungwal fern – *Blench numidicum*: that's good. Some pink finger orchids – the *Caladenia canea* – are also good. The wild parsnip – *Trachymeneincisa* – is full of starch. Wattle pods – nothing wrong with them either. Then there are the *violet*-coloured plants: flax lillies;

geebung, high in vitamin C; lillypilly – *Acmena Smithii*, fruiting right now; the purple banksia' – she glances at the old man huddled in the rear of the cave – 'we can ferment that to make alcohol; more violet flora – the fig of the creek sandpaper. And there's nothing wrong with the mushrooms.'

Chapter 30

THEY CALL IT PARRICIDE

The old man staggers out of the cave, attracted by the smell of cooking. His clothes are rumpled, his mouth's puckered and his face is covered with stubble. He grabs a lump of moss out of the pan and shoves it in his mouth. There's got to be something in that pickled brain of his.

'Come on,' I tell him, 'it can't be that hard to remember. Preferably where we lived but if you can't manage that, something else that might prove useful.'

'Useful for what?'

He goes to pick something out of his rotten teeth, glances across at Sally and thinks better of it. Then, incredibly, coherent sounds emerge. Something's evoked memories. It must be sobriety. He waves at some point in the distance.

'Over there was a commune – Wellsprung or Mainspring or something. It's where Heather lived.' His arm makes an arc. 'Over there was Janice's.' Another arc. 'And Rosie lived there.' He's boasting about the lovers he had when he was married to my mother. 'Past that hill was little Kaska's hut. And –'

'But where did *we* live?'

'Calm down,' Sally says.

'Over there,' he says. 'We lived over there.'

I look in the direction he's pointing and see some trees move in the opposite direction to the wind.

The Australian bush is like life – you don't know you're lost until you're in it and by then it's too late. I took a bearing and there was the landmark of Nimbin Rocks but once we're among the trees both rocks and sun disappear. There's just the bush, us three – and anyone and everyone that's after us.

We're halfway down the hill when the old man starts to develop the DTs. I could nurse him out of it but I'm not in the mood. We need to replenish our water but that means travelling tangentially to any pursuers and the gap would close that much faster. After a couple of hours I accept we're not going to find any water – not this side of the mountain anyway – and we're wasting valuable time looking for it. I motion to Sally to stop.

'We don't know if they've got dogs but in case they have we've got to take to the trees. We only need to be off the ground for a few minutes to lose them.'

'What about him?'

It's late in the afternoon and the old man's breath is coming in short, ragged gasps. He's trembling and he's got a wild look in his eyes. 'I'll climb, you pass him up, then follow and swing across to the next tree. I'll shove him over to you, climb past, you hand him to me and so on.'

She shakes her head. 'Why am I even doing this? I haven't done anything wrong and I'm not paranoid like some people. I should just walk away.'

'So walk away.'

She doesn't.

Wattles are too brittle while gums have high branches and keep their distance from other trees. It's a good thirty minutes before we come across suitable trees for climbing: a group of camphor laurels. I stuff my whitesides in my backpack, collect the other packs and get up the first tree. Below, Sally and the old man are arguing.

'I'm not going.'

'You have to.'

'I don't *have* to do anything.'

I break in, 'If you don't do what you're told, you old bastard, I'll come down and kill you.'

He holds out his arms and the shakes go into remission. He's light but anyone's heavy when they're reluctant and you're hoisting them into a tree. He clings to a branch as Sally climbs after him. After the first tree it gets easier but any dogs after us will have gained ground. I can't hear them but hunting dogs are trained to be quiet. By the time we reach the last tree they'd be less than a minute away. I drop to the ground, drag the old man after me, Sally follows and I put on my whitesides.

'Now we'll split. I'll take the old man and head left while you go right. We'll meet at that stringy-bark over there.'

The old man's the fisherman on the shoulders of Sinbad, the monkey on my back, a burden I'm lumped with. I don't like him, don't want him anywhere near me. He abandoned my mother and my sister and dumped me. The thought of whip-back saplings lashing his face as we plunge through the scrub affords me grim joy. To my right Sally's making for the rendezvous. The dogs won't see the trees move because they're short-sighted, at least that's what the books say.

When I drop him the old man's head hits a rock. I want to pick him up and drop him again but resist the temptation. Sally kneels and checks him while I go over what we're doing yet again. There's a cop logic and I don't have to be Pythagoras to follow it. It goes something like:

1. Identify corpse
2. On basis of motive and opportunity, list suspects
3. Locate and interrogate
4. Arrest and charge.

All of which means that when they find the corpse they'll round up the local hopheads and track down recent arrivals – private vehicles, hitchers, buses. A simple cross-check will show two men and a woman arrived on the 11.30 am bus from Casino a couple of days back and were last seen in the vicinity of the corpse. It's not hard to work out the rest. But someone lifted the body. The Mafia? Ariadne's people? The thugs that killed Damnation? Pandora?

The old man's stopped shaking.

'I don't know how much of your brain's left after a lifetime's pickling,' I tell him, 'but if you don't use what little memory you've got we'll all end up on a murder rap. What happened?'

'When?'

'When you were with – Christ, I don't even know the name of my own mother!'

'Jasmine. It was Jasmine, sweet Jasmine.'

'All right, you've remembered her name, now try and remember more. What happened? And don't say *when* again or I'll kill you. *How* did she die? *Where* did it happen? *Who* was involved?'

'You're accusing *me*!' he shouts. 'You're saying I killed her but how would you know? You were a snively-nosed little brat then and now you're mad. I'm going to call those dogs you reckon are after us. At least with the cops I'll get justice.'

They call it parricide but they can call it what they like. I grab him by the throat. This isn't a dream. The old man's throat's real, an organ by which he sucks air into his lungs to aerate his blood and stay alive. But Sally's strong surgeon's fingers prise my hands loose. Weals stand out on his scrawny neck. The sight fires something in me and I go to grab him again.

'Where is it?' I demand. 'Where's the funny farm?'

He cringes away, rubbing his throat with one hand while pointing shakily with the other. 'It's – over there.'

Chapter 31

MORNING GORY

I don't know where we are – I don't even know where we are in relation to Booby's place. I've taken another sighting and made a mental note of landmarks. In a vehicle it would be a snip but we've only got our legs and if anyone's onto us they'll have the roads covered. Slipping and sliding down rocky slopes between the trees, around spiky bushes, dragging the reluctant old man with us, it's two hours before we reach the place he indicated from the cave – a sloping patch of ground with a tangle of thorns at its centre, a couple of trees and an outcrop of rock. I don't recognise a thing.

'Are you sure this is the place?' I ask him.

'What do you think I am – a bloody dementia?'

I take it as a *yes* and get out the binoculars. They're not much but for the first time in forty years I'm reminded how we used to live. It was the bark hut and tepee phase of Nimbin, when the druggies' god was Aquarius and life was mist and ashes. Forty years on there's not much left, even of that. Lantana, blackberries and morning glory have taken over, some of the clumps as high as –

There are none so blind as those who will not see, my mother used to say. Closely followed by: *Seek and ye shall find.* It was nonsense, even to my five-year-old mind, no more than playground prattle, a witch's curse, a voodoo mantra. Like: *Close the windows or the bats will get you.* Our hut didn't have windows. It's starting to come back to me.

'My mother was stark-staring mad,' I mutter.

'Were there as many bats in your childhood as there are now?' Sally asks.

'I don't know. We saw what our parents told us to see, feared what our parents *said* we should fear, believed what our parents wanted us to believe.' I think of Imogene then I don't think of Imogene. 'That was how things used to be – our imaginings were far worse than any reality.' I swing around to the old man. 'Is this the place?'

He's gone sullen again. 'How would I know?' I lunge at him again, my need to hurt him eclipsing my need to find Pandora. He steps back, a look of fear in his eyes. 'Yeah, this is it.'

A confession obtained under duress is no confession at all but there's nothing else. I can't hear the dogs but that doesn't mean they aren't coming. Someone killed Monica Best and removed her corpse. The cops will have stumbled across it in a shallow grave or someone will have found it for them. Cops feed on death. They can't be far off. They like to be in at the kill.

'You're lying.'

Sally intervenes and the old man decides he's safe again.

'Why would I lie to you, son?'

Forty years on and I'm back at the funny farm looking for my mother. Correction: I'm looking for *who killed her* because that would explain everything. Because I no longer believe she killed herself. The killer could have been – probably was – my father. The *idea* of suicide was something the old man fed to me on the trip to Sydney. The killer could have been Pandora because Pandora dates from my mother's death. Seeing someone kill my mother when I was five would go a long way towards explaining my paranoia. It would also explain Pandora.

The old man was the rough draft but I'm the correcting fluid. Another scrap of memory: our hut was built on a slope so the rain wouldn't turn the floor to mud. Amid her ramblings my mother praised the old man because it was the one thing he got right – he built our pathetic little hut on a slope so the floor would stay dry.

I leave them by the odd-shaped bush – my father huddled in a heap with Sally tending to him – and make my way westward through the waist-high vegetation. I come across a fork in the road and take the left-hand one. *Method detect,* Rube said – *put yourself in situ and relive what happened.* There's something familiar about my surroundings. I stumble across what I'm looking for among the trees.

They're still there, only much bigger now – among them the Moreton Bay fig with roots like pythons. *I'll go and hide,* I'd tell my sister. *All right,* she'd reply. Then I'd disappear, not to return until nightfall. Sophie would still be waiting because she trusted me. Sometimes there were others but mostly there was just us. I ignore the ephemera – dirt tracks, rabbit holes and weeds – and keep an eye out for the more enduring landmarks.

I'm looking for a forest. Not a forest of trees but a forest of totems and a windmill. After forty years most of it will have gone but there must be remnants. That night with my mother and sister turning into skyrockets, I found refuge among a towering array of totem poles. But so far I've found only trees. Then around the other side of the hill – the blind side, the side I couldn't see through the binoculars – I find the shrouded ones. If this isn't the place, I tell myself, I'll kill him. At least I'll have that satisfaction. The cops will get me but they'll get me anyway.

I find an old fence, its posts splintered and sagging, the wire that links them broken and rusted. My jacket snags on barbed wire and I curse the living daylights out of it. My shoes squelch in boggy soil. There's nothing here. How could there be? It's too marshy. I pull away one last shroud …

… to expose one leering face after another, the totems that scared the hell out of a five-year-old kid, a cluster of Easter Island statues with black holes for eyes, made of wood like the fence posts, grey and leaning with age. *Put yourself in that space and time,* Rube said. I'm a kid again and my mother and little sister are burning. *Put yourself in that space and time.* But I don't need to imagine myself anywhere. I'm

here. *You see what you want to see.*
But there's something wrong.

Daylight's fading by the time I get back and there's darkness in my mind. Sally has lit a fire, tearing stuff from the odd-shaped bush in the clearing and putting a match to it to heat up the leftovers. Something registers in my mind. It's not the fire, the smell of cooking mushrooms or even Sally. The old man's curled on the rock like a goanna sucking the last of the day's heat from the sun.

'You look as if you've seen a ghost,' Sally says.

The wind shifts and the smell of cooking wafts across to me. Out of nowhere a figure steals into my brain – a giant figure, real and yet not real. There was a clump of vines around the remains of a windmill but when I dragged them away all I got was a memory – a memory and now this mind-numbing stench. A stench as strong as incense.

'There was a ceremony,' I hear myself say.

Sally busies herself with the pan. 'What kind of ceremony?'

'Something to do with –'

The wind shifts again, blowing the smoke towards the old man. He comes alert and suddenly there's a tension in him yet all that's happened is that smoke blew in his face. They call it the foetal position – knees drawn up, head bowed, hands between thighs. But suddenly there's nothing foetal about him. He's a coiled spring. *Death and transfiguration,* the necromancer said.

'That's it!' I shout, 'I only *thought* I saw a burning windmill because that's what he *told* me I'd seen. And I believed him because he was my father but also because I knew about windmills while I didn't know this other thing. Or didn't want to.'

Sally doesn't take her eyes off the pan. 'You disappear and when you return you're spouting nonsense.'

A vehicle's approaching, the rough road turning the sound of its approach into an alarm.

'Put out the fire!' When I drag the old man to his feet his buttons pop. 'It's February the thirteenth, the day before St Valentine's, and you knew what happened then and you know what's going to happen now. It's a spectre that's haunted you ever since you ran away from here, why you became what you are. *How did she die?*'

'I don't know!' He's backing away from the truth as much as from me. 'I don't remember a thing!'

The car's getting closer. We could hide but they'd see the fire – it's only smoke but that's enough. I let go of the old man and throw the jacket onto the fire. Something's clicked into place. I'm no longer a kid, no longer at the mercy of other people's versions of what happened.

Chapter 32

FINDERS KEEPERS

After the car passes I tell them to stay put, retrieve my coat and gun and go after it. The tracks show that it took the road to the right, the one I didn't take earlier. My foot warps in a rabbit hole and I throw out my hands to break my fall, losing my gat in the process. I scrabble around. It takes a while to find it – too much time. By the time I have it in my hand, the car's well and truly gone.

It's futile but I keep after them. Life's futile but it doesn't stop you living it. And sometimes, like now, it pays off. When I turn a corner, I find the car stopped and two cops standing beside it.

'What would your mother say if she could see you now, in Nimbin the day before Valentine's Day, issuing fire warnings?' one of the cops is saying.

'But that's not what we're doing, is it? We're relieving ourselves. And when we've done that we'll make a routine call on some whackos to remind them we exist then go back to the station and play cards.'

A stone rattles away under my feet and the younger cop spins around, gat in hand. I freeze.

'What was that?'

The older cop calmly zips up his fly.

'You've been in Nimbin too long, pal. You're paranoid just like the rest of them. Put away your gun – in fact put away both your guns. All we're doing is making a routine call. We're still half an hour away, so let's go.'

When I get back to camp Sally's pulled away the rest of the bush, exposing the hut, and made three beds out of biddy bush. It's a long time before I can sleep. Light plays on the walls of the old hut – orange interspersed with yellow and violet. Violent violet, violet violence. Lights – not playing but fighting, fighting for keeps. Finders keepers, losers weepers. The words meant nothing to my sister but when I chanted them she wept because she knew I was rejecting her.

We leave before dawn, the old man waking in unaccustomed sobriety. I clamp a fist over his face in case he tries to call out. It's the second time I've done that – the first being last night when the cops returned from their mission. By then we'd heaped dirt on the fire so again they didn't notice us. There were no dogs – just the car with the diagonal stripes along the side, the red and blue lights on top and two cops inside. All they'd have seen was the hut but it wouldn't have meant anything because they weren't looking for it – all they were doing was checking on a bunch of whackos preparing for St

Valentine's Day.

They'd been no more than an hour – long enough to call on whoever they had to call on but not long enough to do anyone any harm. They were travelling slow which meant they hadn't uncovered anything new. They'd made a routine visit and given their stock-standard warning – *it's summer but you can have your fire as long as you're careful*. I remove my hand from the old man's mouth. I would have liked to keep it there.

'Where are we going?'

'Back to my past.' I indicate the old man. 'Make sure he keeps up.'

There's been a change of clothing – I'm back in grey, Sally's wearing a viridian T-shirt and turquoise-coloured jeans to go with the landscape and the old man's in something similar. She might still dislike me but her attitude's changed. Towards me. Towards the old man. Towards life.

'Come on, Grandpa,' she murmurs.

It's late afternoon. We've stopped, rested, then resumed walking. I'm working backwards from things known – the territory's familiar but only after I've seen it. Déjà vu's like that – no more than wisdom after the event, a murderer's confession. It would have been easy to abandon the old man at the airport or in the hut. Except I still need what he's got locked in that head of his – in the unsafe safe. *Half an hour,* the cop said. Travelling at 20 kilometres an hour over rough terrain, half an hour would mean 10 kilometres. At our current rate of progress it will take us three hours – maybe a little longer.

'You're your bloody mother all over again,' the old man says. 'You'll end up topping yourself, too.'

'What do you mean – *too?*'

'She killed herself.'

'No she didn't. It was a long time ago and I was five.' I'm talking more to myself than to them. 'It was dark, I was scared and I saw what I expected to see. I was a child with a sheet of butcher's paper and a bunch of crayons drawing straight lines to depict a forest. I *thought* they were on a windmill because I *knew* about windmills. I was a kid and saw what I thought I saw. This other thing was too dreadful to acknowledge.'

'You're talking nonsense,' the old man says.

'If I am it's because you brainwashed me.'

'Why would I do that?'

'Because you're guilty – of what exactly, I haven't worked out yet.'

Normally I get at the truth by waving a gun and asking if they care about their loved ones. But I'm well past that stage with the old man. If I pull out the gat it'll be to kill him. I've found the well only to discover it won't give up its water. I make a stab at the truth and bank on him correcting me.

'You killed her because you wanted her out of the way so you could take up with your blonde.'

'But I'd already taken up with the blonde.'

I touch the dolls in my pocket. They're a child's dolls, the kind Sophie used to play with. But why were they where they were and why did I keep them? I know the answer but I don't tell the old man – it's the only ammunition I've got. The sky's occupying that part of the spectrum between cobalt violet and mauve where nearby objects seem distant and far-off ones appear within reach. I'm a child again, seeing the world with a child's eyes again. I nod to Sally.

'Let's go.'

It's late. Sometimes we stayed up late. What am I saying? We *always* stayed up late. There were beds if we wanted to sleep, food when we were hungry and ragged affairs made of rabbit skins if we became cold. We found food where it happened to be, slept when we felt like it and the rest of the time ran around naked. The adults worshipped symbols and the symbol that seemed to work for everyone was fire. We're close enough to smell it now. We stop to rest.

Memory: There was only one source of fire and that was the Mushroom Man. No-one else could keep fire on pain of – I was going to say *death* but stop myself. It couldn't have been death. We were a happy little commune. But I remember that after fire had served its purpose it had to be extinguished. The Mushroom Man sat in his cave like a giant toad. No-one saw his face. Like the bats in my mother's mind, there was a possibility he didn't exist.

There were other kids but many were spirited away. My closest childhood friend, Ace Mollema, left when he was four. *My grandparents kidnapped me,* he said the last time I saw him. *They made a joke of it, calling it kin-napped.* Others followed. And those that were left – me, a couple of boys, a handful of girls – had to cope as best we could. Fantasy helped.

More memories: The adults called the Mushroom Man a name far beyond our childish knowledge. We thought it was *Promises.* I'm off to *Promises,* Mum said, going off with her kerosene stick to return with fire. Only now do I realise what she was saying was *Prometheus* – the name of the god that stole fire.

Chapter 33

LOSERS WEEPERS

The old man has reached a state of awareness and Sally seems to have twigged to something. I can see it in the glances she throws my way. Or maybe that's my imagination again. The weeds didn't exist in my childhood – the hippies must have introduced them in their fruitcakes, scattering the seeds along with the crumbs. Blackberry seeds, lantana seeds, the seeds of that violet-flowered excrescence, morning glory. Anything that could survive.

Sophie had blonde hair and I was so jealous of it that I hacked it off with the scissors. Afterwards my sister looked like a thistle and because of what I'd done I was universally hated. It was my first lesson in criminology – hurting people might make you *feel* good but doesn't necessarily make you *look* better. In fact, when you're found out you look a whole lot worse. After that I made a point of taking care of her. Until the night she died on the windmill. No, *not* on the windmill.

In the mouth of his cave the Mushroom Man was little more than a shadow. If you were lucky you caught a glimpse of the yellowed soles of his feet. People left offerings in exchange for fire. I'd forgotten about him until now – Calvary would call it *Positive Forgetting*. The figure was obscured by the dark sheet of glass placed between me and my childhood. Along with the events of that night.

The dark sheet of glass. Pandora's been with me so long it seems wrong to doubt her but what if the shrink was right? None of the women in my life could be Pandora because of their age, however much I'd like it to be otherwise. Forty years have passed since she first came into my life, a female figure in black, her face a blank slate on which I drew what might have been her features. I knew nothing about her except that she made me afraid. She always appeared when I was at my most vulnerable.

Calvary: *She's a figment of your imagination, the embodiment of your fears. Like the gods of old, she possessed human form and your guilt turned her into a woman. Guilt over your treatment of your sister, guilt caused by your mother's death. But that's all she was — the embodiment of your fears. Because in reality she never existed. If she had existed, she'd have had a lot better things to do than follow you waving a knife. I won't say you're mad because that word's not in my professional lexicon. But your thinking's at best tangential.*

In my mind the old man's mocking me: *Tangential? Give me a break. Why don't we call a spade a shovel and accept that, just like your mother, you're stark, staring mad.*

'Keep moving.'

There's no moon and I find myself half in, half out of reality, only dimly aware of Sally and the old man. I told her to buy black and that's what she's wearing — the kind of clothes ballerinas wear to depict evil — black, skin-hugging leotards, black tights, black sneakers. She's here because I put her in danger. Correction: she's here because *I'm* the danger. Or maybe there's another reason. The world's surreal — the sky's solid while the distant hills, the weed-shrouded buildings and the trees outlined against it are yawning chasms. The old man and the woman are conspiring against me. I feel the fire's heat and as we close in it becomes a conflagration, reaching out of the blackness to engulf us. I stop.

'What's wrong?' Sally asks.

I shake my head in an attempt to clear it. 'We're almost there. I want you both in front of me where I can see you.'

The old man hangs back, reluctant to go on, like he, too, has also remembered. But that's not what he says.

'I'm not going any further.'

'You'll do what I tell you.'

Sally doesn't say anything, like she's one step ahead of me, has already solved the case. What if I rule her out? What if *Sophie's* Pandora? What if my sister escaped the conflagration? And I suddenly realise that I've nursed that possibility – no, *hope*, because it would mean she's still alive – ever since it happened. However malignant she might have become, I'd be happy to the point of delirium to know my sister was still alive. Because I loved her but also because it would be one death I'm not responsible for. I hid while she was burning. But how could I be responsible for my sister's death if she's still alive?

Last seen she was small, blonde and three. Sally could be in her early forties. Which means that the two – no, three: Sophie, Sally and Pandora – could be one and the same. It doesn't explain the figure in the shadows the night my mother died but memories needn't be perfect. I'm back in the midst of my nightmare and shadows dance around the moon.

I blacked out and when I came to I found Monica Best dead. Sally knows her way around fungi and could have fed me anything. But why would she do that? *Because she's my sister Sophie and hates me for what I did or didn't do.* But isn't that like the shrink saying I imagined Pandora – one mad idea replacing another? *Think, dammit, think! You're no longer a child and these aren't shadows.*

'The old man won't go any further – he's says he's tired, thirsty, sick and afraid,' Sally says.

While she's tall, lithe, beautiful and dressed in black. 'And guilty,' I say. 'You forgot *guilty*.' When I take hold of the old man's arm it's a twig, so thin I could snap it. 'You're coming with me and you'll tell me what's locked in that miserable head of yours if I have to kill you.'

I drag him after me and Sally follows and suddenly they're on us, a mass of leaping shadows, figures gesticulating, the past come to life, a world of terror. There's music, the kind that comes out of a loudspeaker, but I'm too busy focusing on the visual stimuli – the fire, the shadows and, closer to hand, Sally and the old man. The wind's blowing away from us and towards the flames – which is why I only caught a whiff of it before. Before I understood there was never any burning windmill. My sister didn't die. There's even a chance my mother's still alive, that I imagined her death, too.

I go weak at the knees. Nothing's as I thought it was. It was a child's world and this is the reality. The change of wind and the chanting bring it back. I was a kid and my mother and sister were in peril. People were dancing and there was a kaleidoscope of colour. I was aware of flames and my sister's mute appeals for help. Because she knew her big brother would always be there when it mattered. There were no Easter Island statues or burning windmill – that's what I imagined to soften the awful reality. But if there was no windmill, how did they die?

Apply free association, another magician's trick, this time that of the shrink. The Mushroom Man wasn't

Prometheus but a magician. The medicine man, bone pointer, shyster, shalyun, shamus. *Shamus: n. Private detective, person pretending to be what he's not – danger man.*

You don't know what you've forgotten until something triggers the memory. I saw my mother and my sister die and after that I ceased to be a kid. Because mothers and sisters don't die, they're there forever. It's why I refused to accept the reality and why I hated my father. What I believed *became* the reality when I couldn't cope with what happened – a reality my father reinforced on the journey to Sydney. But what's happening now triggers the memory. I take out my dead-man's mobile and call the number on the card – the one the man in the white coat gave me. And after that I call the cops.

We're at the pile of rubbish next to Booby's place. Only it's not a pile of rubbish at all but a pyre – from the Greek *pura* meaning *fire*. A funeral pyre. There's smoke and, deep within the smoke as if projected on a sheet of glass, a figure. This is the smoke and mirrors of a shamus. And within that smoke, upon that glass, the giant image of – Pandora. I've found her only to discover she's a wraith, a phantom, a writhing image. And back from the fire in the swirling shadows another figure, a giant in a cloak, a high priest or a god, his arms raised either in benediction or as a threat. The fire's behind him and I can't make out his features. I look back and see something I hadn't seen before, a flaming cross. And on the cross, a naked figure. Even from here I can make out the meaningless words – *TRANNE SOL 10*. But suddenly they're not meaningless at all. I see what's there instead of what I expect to see. It's not *10* but *IO* and the words aren't meaningless but Italian. The words read: *No-one but me.* Meaning: *You're mine.*

Memories overwhelm me. Of a giant in a cave. Of figures dancing around a volcano. Of a small boy refusing to accept what was there before his eyes because it was too terrible to believe, accepting what he was told because it was easier. From a distance I hear my mother's voice chanting, *Cut off their legs.* The smell's intense, dizzying, profound, and sparks dance like sins fleeing from a box. Figures – they seem more like black cut-outs than humans – dance around the flames, contorting like the figure on the cross, waving cups spilling some sort of liquid. The fire's out of control. So are the dancers. I called the cops. Where are they?

But I know where the cops are. *Veni, vidi* but not *vici.* They came, they saw and they cleared out. They had a duty, they did it and they're back at the station playing cards. Local madmen are a protected species – wild but harmless. They're not supposed to be lighting fires in summer but what the hell. The cops aren't here because forewarned is disarmed, this is just another pagan rite and the cops have got better things to do with their time, like playing cards back at the station. Like the cards dealt by one of the naked figures dancing around the fire, the grandmotherly figure that dealt me the Death card while reassuring me: *It's not death but transfiguration.* A grandmotherly figure that's become a virago, its arms outflung, cup raised above its head – the blind necromancer. The figure in the cloak speaks.

'Come unto me, ye unsightly and infirm, and be transformed.'

The smoke forms a screen, like the cracked lounge room wall Aunt Rube screened her old movies on. And on that screen is the figure of Pandora. I trace it back to a smaller one beside the figure in the cloak. Somehow it's been projected – enlarged and terrible – onto the flames. Smoke and mirrors. The smoke wafts towards me and my knees buckle. Memories swamp me. Flames and flood, fire and water, primal elements worshipped by the commune long ago and still revered now. At last I remember. There was no windmill, except the one in my mind, not here, not when my mother and my sister died.

Only this.

Chapter 34

BOOBY TRAP

'In the beginning our souls were wreathed in fire. We are tempered steel and that's what makes us strong.'

'Strong!' chants the crowd as they dance around the flames. 'We're strong, strong, strong!'

Smoke and darkness impair my vision. As in a dream, I see the magician with his arms raised, the contorted figures dancing around him and the fire with the sacrifice on the cross. Above it all the black figure of Pandora, outlined in the haze.

The wizard chants:

But first on earth, as vampire sent,
Thy corpse shall from the tomb be rent,
Then ghastly haunt thy native place
And suck the blood of all thy race.

These are real memories, not the distorted imaginings of a kid. Memories of my mother and sister spinning above the dancers' heads on a burning cross, converted by my childish mind into a windmill because it was something I could comprehend. But houses aren't triangles perched on squares or the Australian bush a bunch of matchsticks. This is reality. It's not what I was looking for. I was looking for Pandora, not an image projected on a screen of smoke, a shamus with his arms raised and a chanting crowd drugged out of their brains.

'I am the darkness and the truth,' intones the Mushroom Man. 'Truth is in darkness, hearken to Pandora.'

'Hail Pandora!'

I'm a child again, hiding behind a totem pole before a burning windmill again. But that's what I imagined, it's not the truth. Because the truth is what's unfolding before me, a scene no five-year-old had any hope of coping with. Which is how they wanted it. They wanted us afraid, needed us vulnerable in order to mould us. *He made you in His image.* They're the words I heard all those years ago – declamation and response. And above it all – shrill and helpless – the pleas of my mother and sister while my father grabs me by the arm and drags me away.

'He's gone!' Sally says.

It's *Walpurgisnacht* with the figure of the Mushroom Man dancing attendance on Pandora and dancing figures dropping like flies. *He changed hands and whisked and rioted like a dance of Walpurgis in his lonely brain.* And the sacrifice. Don't forget the sacrifice.

'Get him!'

It's the wizard shouting and he's pointing at me. I head towards him, a giant figure towering above me and seared in my memory.

'Get him! Bring him back!'

Other voices, my own among them. Because out of the corner of my eye I see the frail old figure entering the flames. I've got a decision to make. Save the old man or go for the shamus. I tear off my jacket and plunge forward, divesting myself of the rest of my clothes until I'm naked like the dancers, a kid again. Only this time I'm trying to save someone. I shove the dancers out of the way as I follow the matchstick figure into the flames.

I'm only dimly aware of the heat, of the incense, of the chanting figure of the shamus, the music, the dancers, the sacrifice. Or the giant, two-dimensional shape in the smoke – Pandora. Or the voice of the shamus and the response of dancers on whom whatever poison he's used hasn't taken effect yet.

'Who are we?'

'We are the indestructible.'

'Can the flames touch us?'

'No, for we can dance upon burning coals.'

The voices of the still-surviving dancers become at one with that of the wizard.

'We must make the ultimate sacrifice to Pandora. We must appease her wrath. Because only then will she be on our side, her anger abated, our protectress.'

'Burn!' the wizard screams.

'Burn! Burn! Burn!' the dancers scream back.

'Kill!'

'Kill! Kill! Kill!'

They're all about me – the ghostly figures that have peopled my mind for so long, the figures of my childhood, my nightmare. The Mafia, grey men with guns, men that might be cops, the blind necromancer, men in white coats and Pandora

Chapter 35

THE FATHER THE BETTER

'Wake up!'

I'm dreaming. An angel is hovering over my head and I'm dreaming. The sky's the colour of violets and I smell the intemperate smell of burning geraniums. There was a night of bleeding angels, of people dying and the contorted figure of Pandora. It's not reality, not the facts. Aunt Rube wouldn't be happy at how my mind worked. *You're a private eye,* she'd say. *You deal in facts. Because if you don't deal in facts you're not dealing.* I try to focus but fail. I can't see.

'Your eyes are burnt,' says the voice of Sally. 'Try and keep them closed.'

'What happened?'

'I'll tell you if you lie still.' The shadows shift as I wait for the voice to continue. 'Forty years ago on a farm in Africa, more than 900 sect members died when their leader dosed them with cyanide. The Jonestown Massacre it was called. Booby was doing a copycat killing and while he was doing it, your father pushed through the dying dancers and entered the flames –'

'I want to hear it blow by blow.'

I already know most of it. When we arrived Booby was ready for us because of the geographical position finders in the dolls – like the ones in the tracker bracelets on Monica and Hélène's wrists. I was led by the nose – courtesy of the murders, the dolls, the necromancer and the smell of the fire. It was just a matter of joining the dots, the kind of picture puzzle children are given to solve. And for the purpose of this game I was a child. Sally worked out the hallucinogens that were fed to the dancers – a mixture of manmade ones and the kind found growing wild. Like children, the dancers saw what they expected to see. Booby used props – prime among them the figure projected in the flames that seemed impervious to fire, Pandora – what he promised the dancers they could become.

'Booby and his wife used smoke and mirrors. The smoke formed a screen on which the figure of Pandora was projected and next to her was the sacrifice.'

'A sacrifice that was already dead – Monica Best.'

'Monica served a twofold purpose. She led us to Booby but she was also a sacrifice. She was long dead but no-one but us knew that. She was what the celebrants expected to see. You, meanwhile, knew who she was and that she was already dead. But the old man saw something else – he saw his beloved wife and a second chance to save her. He dived into the flames and you went after him. Oblivious to the other sect members dying around them, the surviving celebrants went on chanting and dancing. The old man was bringing the corpse out of the flames when the police arrived.'

'Why did he try to save someone he thought was his wife when he neglected to save her all those years ago?'

'As I said, it was his second chance. In his mind, forty years hadn't passed and the dead Monica had become the live Jasmine. He saw what he most desperately wanted so see.'

'Which means he was off his brain on something just like everyone else.'

'I know you're saying I drugged you but, believe me, I didn't. The power of suggestion was enough. The leaves in our campfire might have helped but only by way of arousing memories. The mushrooms were harmless so I think it was the leaves. You were cast back in time to when the sect sacrificed your mother and little sister.'

'So why did my father abandon her?'

'All those years ago your father was faced with that most monstrous of choices: who to save. He chose you. He didn't abandon his wife and daughter – he rescued his son.'

'He came out of the flames.' I look around blindly. 'Is he here? Where are we?'

'We're back in the hut, safe for the moment because no-one knows we're here. After I stopped you killing Booby I tended to your father. He was burnt but, incredibly, still alive – in shock but still alive. He managed to say something.'

'What?'

'He said, *Tell Rainbow –*'

'Tell Rainbow what?'

'He said, *Tell my son I need a bloody drink.* Those were his last words – *Tell my son I need a drink.* Then he died.'

I need to laugh but I also need to cry so I do neither. Private eyes don't cry, not in public. That's why they call us private eyes. But right now laughter's not coming all that easy either. I never knew my father – not until he died.

'How come the cops didn't arrest us?' I ask.

'I told them the truth – that I was a doctor – so they left us alone. They were more interested in Booby and Marsha and saving as many sect members as they could, the blind necromancer and your shrink from the clinic among them. Your father was taken off in an ambulance. I managed to spirit you away and we're safe for the moment but eventually the police will work out who we are and where we've gone and come after us. So as soon as you're up to it – or before if possible – we have to get out of here.'

She gives me something from her first-aid box and I get the impression of a short, disjointed journey, during which I ask, 'What about you?'

'I've decided to stop running. I'm going to tell the Witness Protection people I'm taking myself out of their program. They can make it seem like I died along with all the others. It shouldn't be hard – people see what they expect to see. But that's one question too many because you can no longer cope with the answers.'

'Will I be able to see again?'

'Let's see, shall we? I'm sorry, that wasn't meant as a joke.'

I struggle to sit up but can't. 'I failed to do what I set out to do, didn't I? I didn't find Pandora … But it was you all the time, wasn't it?'

It's the first time in a long while I've heard her laugh and it's birdsong, a full-throated chuckle – all that and more. 'That'd be an easy solve, wouldn't it? Sorry to disappoint you, Rainbow, but no, I'm not Pandora.'

'Then who is she?'

She laughs again. 'I think you know who she is and that you've known all along – you just buried it in your subconscious so you could function more or less normally.'

Her voice becomes teasing. 'I can't tell you any more because you're in shock. I've given you something to make you sleep so your mind wouldn't be able to handle the information anyway.' Her voice has the quality of a late-summer landscape, the perfect landscape for a murder. 'We have a twelve-hour journey ahead of us but you need no longer worry you're being followed. The police have arrested Booby and along with him the Mafia thugs as well as Ariadne's goons.'

'How am I travelling?'

My last thought before I fade is that she misunderstood me when I desperately needed to be understood. Because I already know how I'm travelling. But I've had a good non-life. I've had a child and there's an outside chance she doesn't hate me. What more could a private detective hope for?

I don't remember much about the journey. There was the sound of a car then the rattling of a train but like the forty-five years of my life the journey seemed to pass in a flash. Like they say in the classics I haven't died, I've been reborn. I'm dependent again, waiting for someone to change my nappy.

There was nothing before this moment and I don't know what comes after it.

I just want to sleep.

One day Sister Mildred peels the bandages off my eyes and I can see – blurred images like I'm in the midst of a rainbow in which all the colours have merged into one, turning the rainbow brown. Nothing's distinct and one case dissolves into another. We don't see what's right before our eyes; we see what we want to see and what I see is Sally seated beside me.

'Did you say that all those years ago my old man *saved* me?'

She nods. 'It was his epiphany. Up to then he accepted the sect, went along with what they told him. It was hard not to. Booby and his wife were control freaks just like Ariadne.'

She pauses. 'Then they sacrificed his wife and daughter. It was too late to save them but not too late to save you. He grabbed you and took off. The cops never discovered anything – Booby and Marsha either disposed of the two bodies or made them look like suicides and they were fairly certain the old man wouldn't say anything. But Booby and the woman kept their eye on you – via Pandora. At first Marsha was Pandora – as long as she was young and lithe. And when she grew too old they replaced her with girls from the funny farm – Monica Best, with Hélène Dalmatian as backup. But Monica descend upon me. I identify the figure of the preying mantis, Caligari. I thrust aside one dancing dervish for another to take its place. The dancers still on their feet carry knives and they're raised against me. I hear screams and they're my screams; I see blackened hands and they're my hands. And beyond the hands, beyond everything else, I see the old man emerging from the flames carrying the figure of the woman he's saved.

Only he hasn't saved her because she's dead and has been for days.

blotted her copybook by rescuing you so her days were numbered. She didn't know the doll they told her to give you was – I'm sorry, Booby-trapped. Emitting a signal that told them where you were.'

'And Caligari – where did he fit in?'

'For Ariadne, the sect was a way of laundering people in the same way crooks launder money. The sect was a handy little sideline. It was at the funny farm that she found Caligari – a bright-enough lad but about as qualified to be a psychiatrist as my little finger.'

'So she'll go down along with the rest?'

Sally shakes her head. 'People like Ariadne never go down. They get others to do their dirty work for them and if anything goes wrong they just walk away from the mess they created and start again. A sort of metamorphosis.'

Chapter 36

DOUBLE FUGUE

There are visitors, among them my daughter Sophie – sorry, *Imogene*. 'You'll need surgery, Daddy – *plastic* surgery, not a lobotomy. It can only be an improvement.'

'Thanks.'

'It's your fault – you taught me to tell the truth.'

'So tell me the truth about how your *transfiguration* into a cop's going.'

'The short answer is that it's not. Like your sect, police cadets have rituals – it's a control thing similar to the sect's, only the cadets call them *initiation ceremonies* rather than rites. But their self-defence skills weren't up to mine and as a result I hurt some of them. I was suspended pending an inquiry and after the inquiry I was kicked out. They decided I wasn't suitable material – I was a hairshirt when what they wanted was nice blue serge.'

'What'll you do now?'

'I think you know. In fact, like the identity of Pandora, I think you've known all along.'

When I tell Sister Mildred about Monica a look of anguish crosses her face, to be replaced by acceptance, in the way of any nurse learning of the death of a patient.

'I saw that you worked out she was my daughter – I found you studying those photographs. Yes, I was a member of the sect but I managed to escape. I tried to get Monica to come with me but she insisted on staying. You see they'd already brainwashed her. She was a gorgeous little girl and there was a lot of good in her but she was a time bomb – to me, to you, to them.'

I'm staying at Mildred's until judged fit to return to the real world. It suits us both – she's lost a daughter and I've lost a father. Sally comes around a lot and she's no longer a shrinking violet, if she ever was.

'You're not looking too bright,' she says on her next visit.

'That's what my daughter says.' My sight's nowhere near what it was but I can still make out the beautiful woman perched on the edge of the couch. 'Imogene says no-one will ever look at me again without wincing. But in my line of business that might prove useful.'

'Can you handle the truth?'

The traffic rackets by overhead. I'm not ready to look in mirrors but, yeah, I can handle the truth. In fact, after all these years of living in ignorance I desperately *need* the truth. So I tell her, *Yeah, I can handle the truth.*

To which Sally Kane replies, 'Well, the truth is that you look quite nice to me … And I didn't tell you everything the old man told me before he died. He said that he and his wife – your mother – joined the sect because they were looking for Utopia. At first it was okay – Booby might have been Prometheus but he was also an idealist. But he had to keep control. And as dictators have always found, *real* control depends on fear. People were starting to leave the sect and in order to keep them Booby and his wife upped the bread and circuses.

'It was Nero's Rome all over again. They had a strict policy towards escapees. They *monitored* them. They didn't worry about people like your father – he'd drunk himself into a state of harmlessness. But you were a detective so Marsha visited you from time to time in the guise of Pandora. And when she grew too old they used younger sect members – among them Hélène and Monica. They kept tabs on you, knowing that with a little tweaking they could draw you back whenever they needed to. Which they did when you grew too inquisitive. That was when Ariadne gave "Dr" Caligari two choices – to either lobotomise you or trick you into returning to the funny farm.'

Suddenly I want to exist again; to be a proper father again. Plus something more.

'Go on.'

'Malcolm Booby was the front man, the shamus. He wasn't as young as he looked nor as henpecked as he made himself out to be. As a magician, looking younger was a stroll in the Garden of Eden compared with his day job as some kind of jumped-up tour guide. As was appearing ten feet tall when he wanted to look ten feet tall and scaring the hell out of little kids in order to get them to do his bidding. But that's enough for now.'

I want her to keep talking because there's something therapeutic about her voice. As is her reassuring me that Pandora wasn't a figment of my imagination, that I'm not mad, and not a killer. *You're too close,* Monica Best warned. It might have been a warning to herself as well as to me. Because she got too close and in the end became a risk, which was why she had to die.

'But why did Monica save me?' I ask.

'Brainwashing's an inexact science and Monica's better side cut in. She put on her persona with her mask but without her mask she was still Monica and I believe that she loved you.' An interesting expression crosses Sally's face – even with my imperfect vision I can see that. 'Out of character – that is, *as herself* – she couldn't bring herself to hurt you. Consequently she had to die. When Booby and Marsha succeeded in luring you to Nimbin, Hélène was killed and Monica was recalled. Everything was a set up – Booby "accidentally" meeting us; Booby showing us around while Marsha killed Monica; the phone that was supposed not to work but which Marsha answered; the "lollies" that made us black out while they deposited Monica's body in the bush.'

I've worked out most of it but I like listening to her voice; it's like sunrise on a beautiful day; a day to live for; but now it's my turn. 'Monica was Sister Mildred's daughter. That was the photo I couldn't work out – the one that showed Mildred holding a baby at the funny farm. Mildred escaped – she was wounded in the leg as she ran away – but her rebellious teenaged daughter refused to accompany her. Years later, when Mildred and Monica met up again, Mildred accepted Monica for what she was – a kid who'd been brainwashed but who was still, in part at least, there for her. Monica had lucid moments, one being when she killed the thugs at the refuge and brought me to Mildred's.'

I think about that. 'No wonder I was paranoid. The gunman who was after you was Mafia. But the thugs that tried to kill me at the Three Sisters and the one at Rory's were from Booby's cult. Just as Monica and Hélène were trained to stalk people, the thugs were trained to kill. What I thought was a horticultural experiment was a training ground for killers. *I saw what I expected to see.* Speaking of which …'

I swing my legs over the side of the couch, my bare feet touching the cold floor with the shock of sudden awareness. 'Let's take a cab ride.'

Sally puts in a call for a cab with a bump in it, takes my arm and helps me into the wheelchair. She's a doctor. She knows how it rolls.

The place looks different but that's only because the scales have fallen from my eyes. I no longer imagine I'm being followed because I no longer am.

We're stopped by a new guard.

'I'm looking for answers,' I tell him from the wheelchair.

He blocks the way. 'We're all looking for answers, buddy, but you won't find any here – at least, not on my watch. You're wasting your time and everyone else's. This is private property. So why not leave before you and your companion animal get hurt.'

It's the last bit that does it. 'I'm no companion animal,' Sally says warmly as she pushes the wheelchair over the goon's feet. 'So look out because that means I bite.'

We pass through the entrance and down the hall that I'd been led down before and end up outside a door with a sign on it saying: INTERVIEW ROOM. DO NOT ENTER. We enter.

She holds me while I check under the desk and, after that, behind the air-conditioning. It's an easy check because it was never meant to be made. The air-conditioning vents are speakers; there's a stop/start switch on the windowsill; and when I press the little red button marked PARANOID FANTASY 1, a shadow appears on the wall; PARANOID FANTASY 2 produces a series of voices muttering imprecations like *Kill everyone* and *I hate the world*; PF 3 does things to the lights. While PF 4 results in noises that sound pretty much like people trying to kill one another next door.

In the main building I press another button. To hear a voice like my daughter's saying: *How's he coming along?* To which Calvados replies: *It's a bit like doing a trepan, the surgical procedure where a hole's cut in the patient's skull to relieve pressure on the brain. Your father clams up just when it seems as though we're getting somewhere. We use drugs but he seems resistant to them. It's an act of will, as if he's being tortured and would rather die than divulge his secret.* Then the voice that sounds like my daughter's but isn't – yeah, you hear what you expect to hear – asks: *Can you cure him?* To which the shrink replies: *It depends on the secret.*

A shrink by any name is a shamus.

I nod to Sally. 'Those marks of violence on Ariadne's neck that she said I caused weren't real; they were painted on with something like gentian violet. But they served their purpose, making me doubt myself.' I think about that then I don't think about it. 'Let's go, companion animal.'

I'm not imagining the smile in her voice as she replies, 'Any more of that and you'll be the one wearing the marks of violence. Where are we going, shamus?'

It hurts but I shrug. 'We'll think of somewhere.'

I LOVE YOUSE ALL – WELL, ALMOST ALL

They appeared out of nowhere at the launch of the first Rainbow – two young men brandishing business cards and saying, 'We read your book, we loved it and we want to publish it'. They were Rod Morrison and Jon MacDonald who – together with David Henley – constitute Xoum, the brilliant new publishing group that, in a few years, has beautifully produced all seven volumes in what we tentatively refer to as 'our *first* Rainbow series' – in the hope they will continue to publish us.

Why *us*? Because my late-life flowering as an author wouldn't have been possible without the total dedication and unswerving support of Judith, my wife and helpmeet of six years. In a very real way these books are hers as much as they are mine.

I also owe a debt of gratitude to countless others. First my children who – whether they realise it or not – suffered through having a writer for a father. Then there are those who went out of their way to help. In this category are thriller writer Alan Mills, who inspired me greatly and, with his wife Yukiko, remains a close friend; one of my all-time heroes, legendary Australian novelist Barry Oakley, who I was fortunate enough to have as mentor; author

Leone Britt, who had faith in me even when I didn't; and actor, raconteur and entrepreneur Mike Cody, who not only was ever ready with advice and information but dropped everything when he was needed to go into character.

The other rainbows in my life (my abject apologies to those inadvertently overlooked), in alphabetical order (which serendipitously puts my mother and father first), are: Kathleen and Stewart Boag; John, Jane and Julia Boag; that wonderful wood artist and great supporter (who, I hasten to add, is nothing like his fictional namesake), the real Malcolm Booby; Annie Carter; George and Carol Conomos; Michael and Lorise Doumani; Dick and Fay Hughes; Matt and Jessica Lamb; Lini Lee; Julia and Simeon Legian; Keith and Penelope McConnell; John and Marnie Mason; and Paddy Robinson and the other members of the Sofala-Wattle Flat book group who have provided such great input and friendship.

By way of balance are the fraudsters, liars and swindlers of this world who can't be named but know who they are – the thugs who provide rags like the *Terrorgraph* with their daily cannon fodder; and the crooks I've been close to – people who would sell their own mother down the creek for a shilling. In a way they're the ones to whom I'm most indebted because they provide the basis for that essential noir – the dark clouds without which the creation of rainbows wouldn't be possible.

IF YOU ENJOYED THE FINAL
INSTALMENT OF MISTER RAINBOW,
BE SURE TO CHECK OUT THE
OTHER BOOKS IN THE SERIES.

Also available

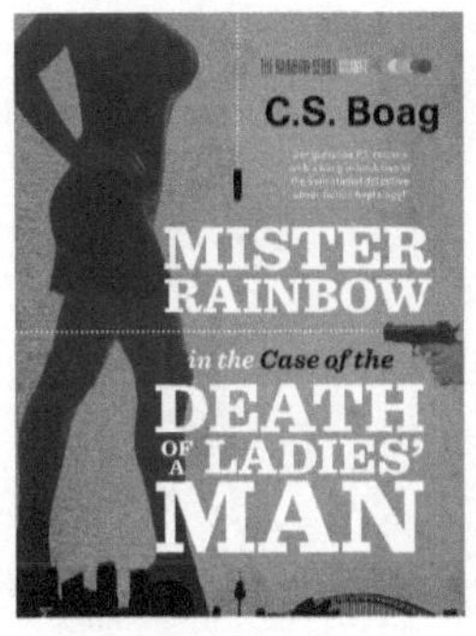

978-1-922057-53-2 (digital)
978-1-922057-54-9 (print)

When Mister Rainbow finds a headless honcho in a
Kings Cross alleyway, the tattoo around the corpse's neck
leaves little doubt as to its identity. Thomas L. Tycho was
everybody's enemy – a trickster, a dirty dealer, and a wide
boy who made the mistake of wide boys the world over – not
making himself narrower when the gun went off.
The killer's identity, however, proves more elusive – as
everybody hated Tommy, anybody could have popped him.
His wife, his girlfriend, and half of Sydney's underworld
all had motive, but Mister Rainbow smells something
fishier than usual, and it's got nothing to do with
what's floating in the harbour …
The Case of the Death of a Ladies' Man is the second novel in
the sensational Mister Rainbow heptalogy.

Also available

978-1-922057-75-4 (digital)
978-1-922057-76-1 (print)
A trip to Paris in the company of a beautiful
dame would be many men's idea of heaven. But a flight to
France with the gorgeous Helen Damnation rapidly
spirals into a journey to hell.
Rainbow's daughter is missing and he doesn't know who's
taken her – or why. Nor does he know where she might have
gone, until he enlists the help of a childhood mate – now a spy
– Ace Mollema. But can he trust the spook? Or the beautiful
dame, for that matter? Above all, can he save the kid?
Sparks fly when Rainbow assumes a temporary identity to
get a passport – and those sparks quickly turn to fire. Can
Rainbow rescue his daughter? And if he does, can he work out
the significance of the Bullets at the Ballet …
The Case of the Bullets at the Ballet is the fourth novel in the
sensational Mister Rainbow heptalogy.